"I'll not have me brother Brian sent to fight. . . ."

"Oh there you are," Miss Sutcliffe said, appearing in the pantry doorway. "It is true, isn't it, what James was telling me, that your brother Brian is too young to be conscripted? I was just mentioning it this morning to Mrs. Lacey. She is so anxious that Master Christopher not have to go into the army, but finish his studies so he can go abroad. And I'm sure that three hundred dollars would be a great blessing in your family."

Katie whirled around. "Me brother Brian's life is not for sale for three hundred dollars. Why should he go and maybe get killed because Master Christopher doesn't want to put his precious skin in danger — even though he thinks the Irish should be happy to go to free the slaves!"

"How dare you speak to me like that?" Miss Sutcliffe said. "You rude, impudent girl! I have a good mind to tell Mrs. Lacey, and you will lose your job, which you deserve to do. . . ."

Katie looked at her and said more quietly, "I'll not have me brother Brian sent to fight, ma'am."

Other Point paperbacks
you will enjoy:

The Quilt Trilogy: A Stitch in Time
by Ann Rinaldi

Wolf by the Ears
by Ann Rinaldi

Sarah Bishop
by Scott O'Dell

My Brother Sam Is Dead
by James Lincoln Collier &
Christopher Collier

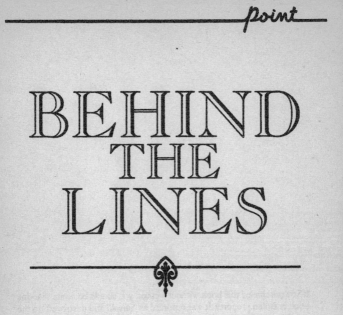

point

BEHIND THE LINES

Isabelle Holland

SCHOLASTIC INC.
New York Toronto London Auckland Sydney

ISBN 0-590-45114-6

Copyright © 1994 by Isabelle Holland.
All rights reserved. Published by Scholastic Inc.
POINT is a registered trademark of Scholastic Inc.

12 11 10 9 8 7 6 5 4 3 2 1   11   5 6 7 8 9/9 0/0

To the memory of Bridget Moore,
whom I knew and loved as Dolly.

Acknowledgments

I would like to thank Ed O'Donnell of Columbia University and Joyce Gold of New York University and the New School for Social Research for their invaluable help.

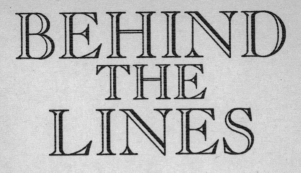

BEHIND THE LINES

CHAPTER ONE

Katie watched the dirty dishwater drain away with mixed feelings. Part of her — the major part — rejoiced that if she had to be a kitchen maid somewhere, at least it was in one of the grand houses on Washington Square that had had the new running water installed. As Miss Sutcliffe, the haughty English governess, deigned to explain to her shortly after she'd been hired, houses built in the 1840's — especially those put up around the square by the wealthy merchants — had their plumbing — or most of it — indoors.

"You are indeed a fortunate girl," Miss Sutcliffe had said on that occasion, pronouncing the last word "gel." "Most girls in your position would be running up and downstairs carrying buckets of used water and — er — waste."

"Isn't that funny now," Katie had said. She'd fastened her blue eyes on the English governess and pushed some escaped black curls back under her kitchen cap. "Since there's none of that lucky running water on the third floor where Josephine and

Dorothea's room is, or the top floor where us common folk live, I still have to carry the dirty pans and slops down the stairs." She'd known, as the words came out of her mouth, that she would be rebuked for her impertinence, and she was.

"*Miss* Josephine and *Miss* Dorothea," Miss Sutcliffe corrected, her voice underlining the *Miss* in each.

"So sorry, I'm just a poor ignorant Irish girl fresh from the bog."

"You will apologize immediately for your impudence, and you will address me as ma'am!"

Katie had opened her mouth, the words "and drop a curtsy as well, no doubt" ready on her rebellious tongue, when Dorothea, the youngest of the Lacey children, had bounced into the kitchen, followed by Mrs. Trevor Carrington, her English grandmother.

Katie had closed her mouth. Not for a moment would she have admitted it, even to herself, but while she controlled her tongue around Mr. and Mrs. Lacey, it was the aristocratic Mrs. Carrington of whom she was more than a little in awe.

As if we didn't have enough trouble with the bloody Ascendency in Ireland, she'd thought to herself as she did, indeed, drop a curtsy. The English pushing us off our own farms. And here, too.

The memory of that scene was with her now as she watched the water swirl out. Yes, it was nice not to have to carry water up and down every floor in the house, or carry dirty dishwater outside to the cistern. But it made bitterer the memory of the filth and stench of Five Points, the slum near the East River docks, which Katie visited every other Wednesday when she went home to see her family. She sighed now and looked up as Mrs. Alberts, the cook, came in.

"Haven't you finished those dishes yet?" Mrs. Alberts asked. "You should have started on the vegetables by now."

"It won't take long to dry them," Katie said.

Mrs. Alberts was a big, powerful woman, not above taking one of the large wooden spoons to Katie's hands if she dawdled. Long ago Mrs. Alberts's parents had brought her from Ireland, but she had married a cockney Londoner who was then the Laceys' coachman, and any loyalty to, or kinship with, the Irish she might have had, had long since vanished, as had any trace of Ireland in her voice. Katie hated her for it, and for the petty cruelties that she indulged in when she was in a temper because the dinner was long and the guests many — a frequent occurrence in a household like the Laceys'.

Taking a dish towel, Katie dried the dishes as fast as she could, stacking them on the table in the middle of the kitchen.

"And you can't leave them there," Mrs. Alberts said. "We're going to have to use that table for chopping the vegetables — which you should have started by now."

"Count to five — or better still, say five Hail Marys," Katie's mother had always said. "With a temper and a tongue like yours, me girl, you'll otherwise find yourself in real trouble!" But she had smiled when she said it, her gray eyes crinkling at the corners.

Katie's mother had died the previous year of the sickness she'd brought with her from Ireland that had eaten her lungs away. Her death, when Katie was thirteen, had changed everything. Before that she'd been a child. Then, when she was fourteen, she had to find a job and contribute to the small and undependable income that her father and her older brother, Brian, made working on the docks. Which meant that Tim, Maggie and Sean, all younger than Katie, were running wild with no one at home during the day to bring them up properly or tell them how to behave. But when Katie begged her father to let her stay home and look after them, he said, "And who's going to pay for their food and clothes, Katie O'Farrell? What Brian and I bring home — when there's work on the docks, that is — won't be enough for three children. Your wages — if you don't spend the money on something foolish — will add just enough to feed them."

Patrick O'Farrell was a loving father, and Katie knew it, even though he didn't have much time for displays of affection, which he called foolishness. It was Katie's mother, Bridie, who'd given her children hugs and kisses. But her mother was no longer there.

And Katie knew that if Da thought she should find work, then that's what she had to do.

"Yes, Da," she had said, swallowing her disappointment.

"It so happens, Katie me girl," her father went on, "that one of the men on the docks is cousin to a man who is groom for a rich family uptown. Maybe he'll know where you can get work."

That was how Katie had become a kitchen maid for the Laceys in their beautiful house on Washington Square.

Katie was torn over what some of her friends called her luck. It was true she now had a bed to herself instead of having to share one with Maggie and Sean and sometimes even Tim. She also had plenty to eat, which was not always true back in the filthy tenement off Baxter Street. But, filthy as it was, it was home, and the people around were fellow Irish and her friends.

Eleven years old before she left Ireland, Katie had grown up imbued with a fierce hatred of everything English. It was the English who had periodically laid waste to Ireland for some seven hundred years, turning the Irish off land that was rightfully theirs, suppressing their religion, and doing nothing to help when the terrible famine came and forced so many onto the roads where they died. These were the stories with which Katie'd grown up. And to make it all worse, her mother, like so many of the others, weakened by years of famine, had become

5

ill. With the potato blight destroying their only food, many of the Irish were too sick and malnourished to make it to the New World or died shortly after they arrived.

Aware that Mrs. Alberts was watching her, Katie went to the cupboard off the kitchen where the vegetables were kept and brought a bunch of carrots and some onions back to the sink. After scraping the carrots, she took them over to the chopping table and, after a quick glance at the clock, started chopping rapidly.

"It's no use your looking at the clock, Katie," Mrs. Alberts said. "As well as the other guests, Mr. Christopher wrote that he's bringing a friend from Harvard for dinner. So there'll be more work than we thought and everybody has to do double."

"It's Wednesday afternoon, Mrs. Alberts. I worked last Wednesday, so it's my afternoon off now."

"There won't be a day off for you today," Mrs. Alberts said. "You'll have to wait another week."

Katie put down the knife. "I can't. I have to get home to see after Tim, Maggie and Sean."

"And how well do you think Tim and Maggie and Sean will do if you lose your job? They'll go hungry, won't they?"

Katie stood for a moment fighting to control her anger. She counted to five and then counted again. Mrs. Alberts, of course, had the whip hand and they both knew it. Jobs for untrained girls were hard — if not impossible — to get. As everyone kept telling her, she was lucky. The numbers of girls no older than herself who were begging on the streets, or selling themselves as prostitutes, attested to that. But the thought of going another week without checking how things were at home — Had the children washed themselves? Was the small kitchen relatively clean with some coal nearby, or was it filthy with the fire out and no coal or wood with which to make a new fire? — made Katie's life even more difficult. But, of course, Mrs. Alberts was right. She could not risk losing her job.

Finishing the last onion with a final snap of the knife, Katie went quickly over to the back door.

Mrs. Alberts turned her head. "And where do you think you're going?"

"To the outside larder. We need some more vegetables."

"We have quite enough here!" But Mrs. Alberts was talking to air. Katie had opened the back door and run to the mews where the family coach and horses were kept and where the overflow of household items was sometimes stored.

Katie knew Mrs. Alberts had enough vegetables, but she had to get away for a few minutes to calm herself.

As she slipped through the gate into the mews, a small tan mongrel flung himself at her.

"There now, Paddy!" She bent down and gave

the dog a hug, got her face licked in return, and felt much better.

It was amazing how much this skinny puppy with his playful ways had come to mean to her. "No, it's no use going on like that," she said to Paddy who, encouraged by her hug, was trying again to lick her face. "I don't have anything for you." She stroked his sides where each rib stood out. "But I'll get something for you, I promise."

"Come on, you! Get out of here!" Carson, the new coachman for the Laceys, aimed his boot at Paddy's ribs. Fortunately, Paddy was able to turn quickly, but the metal toe caught the dog on the side and he gave a painful yelp.

Katie shot to her feet. "Stop that, you brute. He's not doing anything to you!"

"He's in the stables and he's got no right to be there. He's nothing but a mongrel!" And Carson raised his foot again.

But Katie had pushed Paddy behind her and was holding him there. "He's doing you no harm. If you hurt him I'll . . . I'll tell the master." That was a wild charge Katie had just dreamed up. She'd rarely even seen Mr. Lacey, let alone spoken to him.

"And he'd tell me to get rid of him, you stupid girl," the man said.

"He doesn't like people who're cruel to animals," Katie said.

"And so he's been confiding to you how he feels about such things?"

Katie could feel her cheeks burn. "I heard him say it at dinner when I was there handing something to Bertha."

"They'd never let you in the dining room," Carson said, scorn in his voice. But he turned and walked away.

And what happens to Paddy when I'm not here? Katie thought.

Paddy, who was young and silly and didn't know yet how to avoid people who'd harm him, had only been seen in the mews for the past day or so. Where he came from no one knew. But he was a far cry from the fine, pedigreed dogs owned by the Grenvilles and occasionally seen in the mews when they'd followed Master William or Mr. Grenville on the way to their horses.

The dog gave another whimper and Katie bent down to stroke him. "You're a silly dog," she said to him in a low voice, and gently touched his side. This time the whimper was louder.

"Hush now!" Katie said, and put her arm around him.

Part of her feeling for him was rooted in her memory of an earlier Paddy, also a mongrel puppy, back in Ireland. She had no idea where he came from and, of course, they couldn't begin to afford feeding him. But her mother loved animals and would occasionally — when her husband was not watching — give him a bit of her dinner. Katie's last memory of that Paddy was his small form trying to keep up with them after they'd been driven from their farm and were on the road to get the boat in Dublin. Someone had lent them a ride in a wagon and Katie's mother begged her husband to let them take the little dog with them. But he refused, so Katie and her mother watched as the puppy fell further and further behind and finally stopped, his sides heaving. They never saw him again.

Katie sighed, thinking of that earlier mongrel. The two dogs were quite different, really. The one in Ireland was gray and white and a bit older and bigger and shaggier, and probably, she reassured herself, better able to take care of himself.

If she left this one now, after what had passed between her and the groom, Paddy would be either driven out of the mews or killed. And there was no use appealing to Mrs. Alberts. She didn't bother with favors for lesser beings. And Katie knew that both she and Paddy were definitely lesser beings. What could she do with him?

What she ought to do was go back into the kitchen and forget about Paddy. Staying out here would do her no good at all. And she was certain to get her hand smacked for loitering outside when she should be helping with the dinner.

But she was also quite certain that if she left Paddy now he'd be dead or gone by the time she might be able to come out here later and she'd never again see him alive. Where did he come from? Did somebody somewhere in this fine square own him? But she knew the answer to that. If any responsible person owned him, he wouldn't be in the starving condition he was in.

She stared down at the mongrel who was sitting on his backside, staring up at her. "What am I going to do with you?" she muttered.

As clearly as though he were standing beside her, she could hear her father's voice. "Your first mistake, me girl, was feeding the wretched dog yesterday. If you hadn't, he'd not be back here today."

And she knew it was true. Yesterday she'd come out for a breath of air when Mrs. Alberts was taking her midafternoon rest and she'd found him, tail between his legs, running down the mews from some boys who were laughing and throwing stones at him.

Promptly, without thinking, she'd picked up the stones and thrown them back at the boys and told them she'd get the men after them if they didn't get out of the mews. Then, because she was carrying some of the garbage from the luncheon table, she'd put food from the plates down in front of the dog, who'd gobbled it all up.

Suddenly she heard Mrs. Alberts's voice from the back door. "Katie! Katie! Where are you? Come back here at once!"

If she didn't get back she'd be dismissed. There was no question about it.

"You want me to take him, miss?"

It was a voice she wasn't used to. Katie looked up. A small, youngish black man was standing on the cobblestone passageway in the middle of the mews. She'd seen him before, and wondered what he, a black man, was doing there, but she certainly hadn't spoken to him. Thinking he might be an escaped slave from one of the slave states she'd heard about, she said, "And what would the likes of you be doing with him?"

He stiffened. "What do you mean — 'the likes of me'?" He looked her up and down and added, "I suppose you being Irish don't know any better!"

"I'll have you know — " Katie flared back when suddenly Carson stalked into the mews from University Place.

Paddy, seeing the enemy, ran forward, barking.

Carson gave a roar and aimed a kick at him.

Both Katie and the young man dived towards Paddy. Katie picked him up and stood facing Carson. "You rotten coward!" she yelled at Carson. "I'll tell Mr. Lacey!"

"You do that," Carson sneered. "He'll likely pay me to drown him."

"He would not!" Katie yelled.

Carson muttered under his breath and lurched towards the stable.

As the young man started to walk away, Katie noticed that he had a pronounced limp, as though one leg were much shorter than the other. "Don't go," she said.

He turned. They stared at one another.

12

"Where would you take Paddy?" Katie asked.

"To the Grenville stables. I work there as a groom." He turned and waved in the direction of a stable at the other end of the mews.

Katie knew through kitchen gossip that the Laceys and the Grenvilles were friends. "Won't the other grooms or the coachman mind?"

He shrugged. "I don't think so. Anyway, I have a room over the stable, and the dog can stay there."

He spoke well, Katie thought, although he had a funny accent. But then the rich Protestant people in New York — the kind who lived on Washington Square — said that the Irish had funny accents, too. And there was no place for Paddy with her. She had to be friendly, whether she liked it or not. She swallowed. "I'm . . . I'm sorry if I gave offense."

He gave a half smile. "All right. I guess I am, too."

"If you'd take Paddy just for a while, I'll try and find a place for him, and I'll somehow get food to feed him. But you have to watch out for Carson. You saw just now what he tried to do."

"Yes, I know Carson. He gets drunk and mean."

"Katie — you get back here right now!" Mrs. Alberts's voice rang out from the Laceys'.

"I have to go now," Katie said. Quickly she leaned down and patted Paddy on the head. "Be a good dog," she said, and ran back through the gate. The last things she heard before she went through the back door were Paddy's protesting whines as his face pressed against the gate and the black man's voice saying, "Now Paddy, come along with me. Come on now! You can see her tomorrow."

"I'm coming now, Mrs. Alberts," Katie said, as she opened the door and prepared herself for the onslaught.

CHAPTER TWO

Katie washed and chopped her vegetables, keeping her head down and her attention on what she was doing, while Mrs. Alberts's voice rose and fell.

"And if you think we couldn't walk out into the street and get a girl who's just as good as you — probably better — then you'd better think again! It just so happens I have a niece who'd be fine for the job."

Katie concentrated on the potatoes she was peeling and slicing, trying to drown out the cook's hateful voice. She'd heard about the niece before, but hadn't believed she existed. It was the kind of threat the cook would make to keep her on her toes. But then Bertha, the housemaid, had told her it was true. "And jobs are scarce," Bertha had said. "So watch yourself. She'd love to put her in your place." Remembering the niece had helped Katie — sometimes — keep her tongue between her teeth.

When she found her attention focusing on what the cook was saying, she switched her thoughts to Paddy. Just thinking about the way he rolled on his back, his paws up, waiting to have his tummy scratched, made her feel better. She hoped the man lived up to what he promised, letting Paddy share his room. If he didn't — but Katie didn't like to think about what might happen to a small stray animal like Paddy. Why she cared about animals the way she did she didn't know — unless, of course, it was because her mother had.

"There are people starving in the streets, Katie O'Farrell — Irish boys and girls, their parents dead and nobody to feed them, and here you're going on about some wretched cat or dog! It makes no sense at all!" Patrick O'Farrell's voice was clear in her head. He'd said those words one night when he'd found she'd brought home a kitten and was giving it a little milk. He pulled the kitten from her hands, walked down the tenement steps and she never saw it again.

"Ma loved Tabby, remember, Da?" she said to him once.

"Yes, and she gave it food she should have had herself. Don't talk to me about that!"

And Katie didn't dare speak of it again. The day after the funeral mass for her mother, Tabby disappeared. Katie had looked for her all over, but never found her. And she couldn't bring herself to ask her father. He was devastated over his wife's death and sometimes, especially when he came home late after being in the saloon, in an unpredictable temper. But Katie always remembered her mother's face when

16

she stroked Tabby and the way Tabby rubbed her head against her mother and purred.

"Listen to her, Katie," her mother said often. " 'Tis a beautiful sound! I think she has the loudest purr in the city."

That evening, somewhat to her surprise, Katie was told to tidy herself and comb her hair, because Bertha was sick and had been sent up to bed.

"What's wrong with her?" Katie asked Mrs. Alberts.

"Nothing that's any concern of yours," Mrs. Alberts said. "Now get yourself ready." So Katie had to help out in the dining room, not waiting on table, of course, but serving the plates and handing them to James, the footman.

In a brief lull before the flurry of dinner, Katie slipped upstairs to see how Bertha was faring. The housemaid had always been kind to her, often deflecting Mrs. Alberts's remarks, and Katie felt grateful. She and Bertha shared the second attic, but Katie hadn't been upstairs since getting up, and while she knew that Bertha was feeling poorly, she'd been too busy to notice anything beyond that.

When she got up there, Bertha seemed to be asleep, her face almost as white as the pillow. But as Katie approached the narrow bed, she opened her eyes.

"How are ye, Bertha?" Katie asked quietly.

"Not so good. I feel that sick and dizzy!"

"I'm sorry," Katie said. "Is there anything ye'd like me to bring you?"

"No, Katie. Thanks. I couldn't keep anything down. Are you to help James in the dining room?"

"Yes."

"Well, he can be sharp, but don't let him fuss you. Just fill the dishes and hand them to him." She closed her eyes.

Katie paused a moment, then crossed to the washstand where she dipped her washrag into the pitcher, rung it out and took it over to the bed. Folding it, she placed it on Bertha's forehead.

"Thanks," Bertha whispered.

Katie touched her on the shoulder, then slipped downstairs and readied herself for the dining room.

Although she wasn't about to admit it, Katie was pleased to be helping James serve. She disliked and disapproved of everything that the Laceys and their friends represented: They were Protestant, Republican and of English ancestry. They were rich and, to her way of thinking, showed off their riches in the faces of the desperately poor. But, in spite of all that, she did, when she had the opportunity, enjoy listening to what they had to say. They talked of a world she could barely imagine — of balls and governors and universities and travels and of the war now being fought somewhere in the South.

"The Union army's going to have to put up or shut up," one of Mr. Lacey's guests said that night.

"Lee is pushing them hard, and he's a better general than Meade."

Katie, who was busy putting pieces of roast chicken on a plate, wondered who Meade was. She'd heard about Lee. According to her father he was the commander of the Southern army. "And a rare fine fighter he is," Patrick O'Farrell had said. "He'll teach the damn Republicans and that soft-headed man in the White House to stay out of their affairs."

Patrick was an ardent Democrat and felt the war was a waste of time, except, of course, that it supplied pay and food to young Irishmen who signed up in the Union army.

"Yes," Katie had said doubtfully, thinking of some of the conversations she'd heard about in the Lacey household. "But slavery isn't right, Da."

"No, it isn't. And we should know!"

"But the Irish weren't slaves."

Patrick's face had turned red. His blue eyes had blazed. "At least the Southern plantation people *feed* their slaves — after all, the slaves are their property! Why shouldn't they? The English landlords, far from feeding us, turned us off our land and stole our food — our corn and pigs and cattle — and shipped them over to England. And when the famine came and we were starving they pushed us out to die. Do you think that's better?"

"No, Da. Of course not."

"Then don't talk so foolish. This war's got nothing to do with us, Katie. And let me tell you something. The talk in the pubs is that if the South loses, and the slaves are freed, then they'll all come up here and take our jobs, because the hypocritical Republicans can get away with paying them even less than they pay us."

There were five guests tonight. Mr. and Mrs. Lacey, of course, sat at either end of the table. Mrs. Carrington sat in the middle of one side. Master Christopher was there, as was another young man his age. And there were two other couples.

As the talk centered on the war, it was obvious that everyone at the table except the man who'd spoken before was a Republican, a supporter of President Lincoln, and a believer in the Northern cause. The same man said now, "The North has more industry, which means more weapons, more money and a bigger army, and it's still not winning. Lee's invaded the North. He's up in Pennsylvania right now. There'll be a battle soon and I'd lay odds Lee'll win."

Good, Katie thought. And, as she hurried to keep up with the footman who was taking plates from her and handing them around, strained her ears to hear what anyone would reply. By the silence that followed she guessed that, whoever the guest was, he was certainly alone in his opinion.

As she turned to put a piece of lamb on a plate, she glanced quickly at him. He was a lean man with reddish hair. Almost, she thought, he could be an

Irishman, and then dismissed it. The only Irishman who'd be here, sitting at the Laceys' table, would be the other kind, a Protestant.

"I'd take your odds," another voice said almost belligerently. Katie glanced up quickly and saw the speaker was Master Christopher. "Meade'll wipe up the floor with him."

The red-haired man gave a satiric smile. "The way McClellan did, Chris?"

"The Union forces needed a while to assemble themselves," Mr. Lacey said. "But the South can't win. And must not."

"If England decides to help them out, it can. It can break the blockade of Union ships and bring them much needed supplies. And the Union is beginning to lose some of the men whose period of enlistment is over."

"What they should do," Master Christopher's guest said heatedly, "is institute the draft."

"If you feel so strongly about it, why haven't you joined up?" the red-haired man asked.

"Both Stephen and my son are at university," Mrs. Lacey said quickly. She was a frail-looking woman with a pretty, rather anxious face.

"Katie, watch what you're doing!" James's furious whisper snatched back her attention.

She glanced at the footman. "Yes, all right." If he told Mrs. Alberts about her wandering attention, she'd be in more trouble than she already was. Quickly she put carrots and onions on the plates. As she turned away, she became aware of someone watching her, so she glanced up and saw that it was Mrs. Carrington. Her heart sank. In her weeks of service in Washington Square she'd been in plenty of trouble with Mrs. Alberts and Miss Sutcliffe but, as far as she knew, she had never displeased any member of the family. And of all of them, Mrs. Carrington was the most formidable.

Just before she went to bed that night she put a few bits of food from the dinner plates in a piece of newspaper and slipped out the back.

"And where do you think you're going?" Mrs. Alberts asked.

This time Katie was ready. "As I'm sure you know, Mrs. Alberts, the water — the running water — doesn't go up as far as the servants' floor. So I thought I'd just go to the privy outside before bed."

"Funny you haven't done that before." The cook's eyes slid over her. "And what's that in your hand?"

"Just some rubbish James asked me to throw out." Luckily, he was not there to hear her. Mrs. Alberts slammed a couple of kitchen drawers shut and Katie held her breath in case the older woman would demand to see what "the rubbish" was. But the evening had been arduous, and Mrs. Alberts was plainly tired and ready for bed.

"Well, be sure the door is locked when you come back in. Now don't forget!"

"No, ma'am," Katie said.

She waited till she heard the cook's heavy steps mounting the stairs. Then she slid out the back door and down to the gate into the mews.

It was dark by now, although the mews itself was lit by gas lamps and a few flaring torches.

Katie opened the gate. There was a short yelp, then a small body flung itself at her.

"Are you all right, then?" Katie whispered. She ran her hands over Paddy's sides and felt him shrink against her when she touched his injured rib. "The rotten brute!" she said aloud. Then she put down her bundle and opened it.

There was nothing wrong with his appetite. He wolfed down every last scrap of lamb and vegetables.

"There's a good boy," she whispered.

After he was finished, she sat down on the mounting block and patted her lap, wondering if Paddy had ever seen the gesture and knew what it meant. Evidently he did. The next thing she knew he'd jumped up onto her thighs and was trying to lick her face. "There now, all right. You're a good boy, but you have to get down soon." After a minute or so he quieted down and sat on her lap. In the dim light of the gas lamp she sat there for a while, stroking him. Every now and then he'd reach up and try to lick her chin. Katie knew there was no way she could explain to her father — or even her sister and brothers — how much his affection meant, what a hole it filled, although Ma would have understood.

"I wonder where your friend who's supposed to be minding you is," she said to Paddy, and at that moment heard the uneven sound of limping footsteps approaching.

"Oh, he's with you!" The man sounded relieved. "I was working in the stable and when I got home to my room, he was missing. The door doesn't have a proper lock, so he can get out."

"You mean he can get out when Carson is here?"

"When we're both inside I have a bolt I can lock it with, not that it's that strong. But when I'm not there, there's no way I can lock it."

The funny part was, Katie found herself thinking, he talked more like the Laceys and their friends than such Southern blacks as she'd heard, and certainly more than the Irish did.

"Where d'ye come from?" she asked.

"Here."

"So you aren't a slave?"

She could see him tense. "New York isn't a slave state," he said stiffly.

"Sorry," Katie said. "I didn't mean to cause offense."

"My mother was a slave," he said after a minute. "She brought me up from Virginia through the Underground Railway."

"Did she get a job here?"

24

"Yes." He paused. "With a man who taught at Columbia College. He was connected with the Underground Railway." He leaned over and patted Paddy. As he did, something heavy in the pocket of his long jacket fell out.

Katie was astonished to see it was a book. Bending down she picked it up off the cobblestones and peered at it. She recognized a few of the letters on the front, but not enough to know what the words said. As she stared at it, the implications of it being in the groom's pocket sunk in. Finally she said, "D'ye read?"

"Yes. Mr. Lowell, the man my mother worked for, taught me."

She pointed to the letters on the front of the book. "What does it say?"

"It says, *Narrative of the Life of Frederick Douglass*." After a minute he went on. "He — Frederick Douglass — was a slave before he ran away. This is about his life as a slave."

Katie was stunned, and then humiliated, that he could read when she couldn't. Although her mother had known how to read, she'd been too busy, even at their small holding in County Meath, and then too ill, to teach her. And, of course, with her mother's illness, Katie herself had to stay home and work. After that they'd been on the roads to the ferry to Liverpool and then on the ship coming over. Katie pushed her mind away from that terrible voyage. Her mother's illness had gotten far worse, there'd been very little food and the conditions where they slept far below the decks were a nightmare. And then, two years after they arrived, her mother died.

"But you work for the Grenvilles now," she said. "What happened to the man who taught you?"

"He died." There was a pause. "He was killed at the Battle of Bull Run."

"Bull Run?" Katie thought for a moment. "You mean in the war going on now?"

"Yes."

"That's too bad," Katie said.

"Yes. It is."

There was a question Katie wanted to ask, but she wasn't quite sure how to go about it. The only men she knew who were in the Union army went for the pay and the food. If you weren't that poor, and weren't one of the professional officers, like the generals, then why would you be fighting? "Was he one of them generals?" she asked now. "The ones who're running the army?"

The man grinned. "No. He went into the army because he wanted to fight the Southern slaveholders. He was an abolitionist."

Lord save us! Katie thought. The people her father and his friends disliked almost as much as they disliked rich Protestant Republicans. And he could read but she couldn't. She felt her anger rising, and then looked down at Paddy, snoring gently on her lap. She swallowed. "Will ye be going to your room soon for the night?"

"Yes. I'm going now. I came down to this end looking for Paddy."

"I'm beholden to you," Katie said, and heard how stiff she sounded. "Here, Paddy, go with — " She looked at him. "Beggin' your pardon, but I don't know your name?"

"Mr. Lowell named me Spartacus. But Mammy always called me Jimmy."

"Sparta — ? That's a funny name," Katie said.

"It was after a slave who fought for his freedom," the man said. He looked at Katie. "Back a couple of thousand years ago. Mr. Lowell taught Latin and Greek at the College and he knew about things like that."

"How old were you when your mother brought you up?"

"About four."

"So what should I call you?" Katie asked.

"Why don't you call me Jimmy?"

"All right. Thanks."

"And what is your name?"

"Katie. Katie O'Farrell."

They looked at one another for a moment. Katie wondered if Jimmy knew how most Irish felt about the blacks. And then knew somehow that he did. How could he not? There were fights in the streets and in the pubs about it all the time.

"All right, Paddy. Go with Jimmy." And she lifted the little dog off her lap. He made a slight whimpering sound and tried to jump up and lick her face.

"No, you're going to have to go with Jimmy," she said firmly.

Jimmy reached into his pocket. "I brought this," he said, and pulled out a length of rope with a loop at the end. "I thought I might put this around his neck."

"It won't choke him, will it?"

"No. I can fix it so it won't. But he might not want to go with me and if somebody came after him, I'd have no way to get him upstairs."

"All right." She watched while he slid the loop around Paddy's neck and then closed it a little and quickly made another knot. "Come along, Paddy," he said.

Katie bent down and patted him, then ran back through the gate into the Laceys' garden. "Thank you," she said to Jimmy, then went quickly up the steps into the kitchen so that Paddy would go with him.

When she went upstairs half an hour later she checked to see if she could do anything for Bertha. But Bertha was asleep. In the flickering light of the candle Katie held, Bertha's face shone wet with perspiration. Of course it was July and hot but Katie couldn't help remembering the wet sheen that shone winter and summer on her mother's face in the last year of her illness.

When she to bed she resolved that next Wednesday when she went home she wouldn't tell her father anything about Paddy — or Jimmy.

28

CHAPTER THREE

Katie managed to get home the following Wednesday. It was a long walk from Washington Square to the Lower East Side, and as she got nearer to Baxter Street the tenements grew narrower and the streets meaner and dirtier. She was used to seeing pigs foraging in the piles of garbage as she drew nearer home and to stepping over the dirty, smelly water running down the middle of the cobblestones. It was home and these were her people and the Irish accents around her were welcome to her ears. Still, the filth and the stench were a shock after the tidy, clean streets around Washington Square, especially since she'd not been back home for three weeks.

But she hated herself for drawing the comparison, and reminded herself that these were her friends and the people back in Washington Square with all their advantages were her enemies.

A boy of about her own age, pretending to be reeling from shock, said, "If it isn't Katie O'Farrell! Has she come slumming now to visit us from her fine family in Washington Square? And do you make your proper curtsies to her ladyship if she lowers herself to talk to you?"

"It's a pity you don't spend more time looking for decent work and less in the pub, Tommy McDermott," Katie said sharply.

"Ach, it's a good job I have now, Katie," Tommy said, grinning. "I'm a messenger for the club."

"Which meets in the saloon and where you get your drinks," Katie snapped. She knew about the political clubs of the local wards because her father talked about them.

"So you have joined the temperance society like the good Protestants you work for?"

"No, I have not. But I can see you've been at it already and it being only two o'clock."

"Ach, they've had a meeting all morning and I've been running messages to some of the other wards. Are you too grand for us now, Katie O'Farrell?"

He smiled at her, but it was not a smile of friendship. Once before when he'd been taunting her, her brother Brian, coming up from the docks at the other end of the street, had swung him around and given him a black eye and a swollen lip. Tommy had never forgotten it. He usually made quite sure that neither Patrick nor Brian was anywhere within earshot when he baited Katie.

"So tell me now, Katie — "

But Katie had pushed past him and was walking quickly up the garbage-strewn street toward her own tenement. Maggie, eight, and Tim, ten, were playing with other children from the building, shrieking and laughing and pushing at one another.

"Maggie, Tim," she said, and waited for them to run over.

"Are ye back from the grand house now, Katie?" Tim asked. "Ye didn't come last week and Da wondered what had happened to you."

"They had a big dinner and the housemaid was sick, so I had to help out in the dining room."

"Did you bring us anything to eat?"

Once or twice, when Mrs. Alberts was occupied elsewhere or taking her nap, Katie had been able to wrap a few things from the larder in a dish towel and bring them to her family, always returning the dish towel the next day. She did it though she knew other maids who'd been caught doing that had been dismissed as thieves. But since the advent of Paddy, Katie was fairly sure that Mrs. Alberts was onto her smuggling leftovers out to the mews. So because of him she hadn't dared take any today. Her conscience smote her. What would Ma have said about her putting a dog ahead of her brothers and sister?

She'd understand, Katie told herself.

"I'm sorry, Maggie, Tim. I wasn't able to get any."

"That's a crying shame!"

"Next time!" She looked around. "Where's Sean?"

"He's with Father Lavin, being shown how to be an altar boy."

"Oh. That's good!" She worried about Sean, who was almost too young when his mother died to be able to remember her. Because of this, and because he had no memory of their family life in Ireland, he was different from the other two, more distant, less obedient, a little wilder. Perhaps Father Lavin would be a good influence here. He was an austere disciplinarian, an ardent nationalist for Ireland and a hater of everything Protestant. Katie, who had all the family prejudices against the Anglo-Protestants, was the only one now who had much to do with them. Although they could make her as angry as they did the other members of her family, she was forced (sometimes) to admit that they were not all alike, that, like the Irish, they differed from one another. She found herself suddenly thinking of Mrs. Carrington, and then pushed the thought away. Whatever could she, an Irish servant, a kitchen maid, have to do with that grand lady of wealth and education?

She was about to push open the scarred door to the tenement when her eye was caught by a starving, mangy-looking dog, its tail between its legs, gobbling up food from a pile of garbage and trying to avoid a bigger pig doing the same.

It reminded her of Paddy. Mrs. Alberts, angry that she couldn't keep Katie from taking her afternoon off, had kept her washing, drying and chopping up to the moment she left. There'd been no chance to gather up food left after lunch and take it out, which meant that Paddy would be hanging around the back gate. That also meant he might run afoul of the coachman. Sighing, Katie sent up a prayer to St. Francis, patron saint of animals, that Jimmy had somehow found food to feed him, because unless she could find some before she returned, there'd be no hope of getting any tonight.

"Are ye coming up, Katie?" Maggie said, holding the door open.

"I am that."

Katie cooked dinner, consisting of potatoes and a piece of fish from one of the fishing boats, for her father, Brian, and the three children.

The children kept up a constant chatter, mostly teasing Sean about his new duties as altar boy.

Katie smiled at him. "I can see you as a priest already, Sean." And she put an extra potato on his plate.

Sean blushed. "Ach, now, Katie," and pushed the potato into his mouth.

Brian grinned, "Now don't frighten the lad, Katie. You don't want him to drop the holy wafer!"

Katie was supposed to be back at Washington Square before nine, or she would find the kitchen door closed and locked. This meant she had to leave the tenement no later than eight-thirty.

At dinner the next night Katie was again passing dishes because Bertha was sick once more. She was far too busy to listen to what was being said until

Master Christopher's voice, clear and carrying, caught her ear.

"They'll be drafting men of my age, and Stephen and I think it's high time anyway to join up."

"You don't have to go, Chris," his mother said quickly. "You can get somebody else to go in your place. We can pay three hundred dollars. Isn't that what the draft officers said? Three hundred dollars? Then you can go on with your schoolwork."

"But I want to go. I think we ought to fight for the Union, just like President Lincoln says."

"I'm proud of you for feeling that," Mr. Lacey said. "I know we're all very much for abolition." He paused and glanced at his wife. "But your mother is right. Three hundred dollars is cheap enough to give you time to finish your thesis and then do the research work you're planning in England."

"But — "

"Chris! You told me you didn't want to go," Dorothea said. She and Josephine were sitting on either side of Mrs. Carrington.

"I never said that," Christopher said angrily. "What Stephen and I said was that they'd better institute a draft because so many of the men who'd enlisted wouldn't be coming back when their enlistment was over. Anyway, what are you two doing down here at the dinner table? Why aren't you having tea upstairs with your Miss Sutcliffe?"

"Suttey had to go see her sister who's sick," Josephine said.

"Ill, dear," Mrs. Lacey said.

"There's no reason why you should go, Chris," Mr. Lacey said. "Not when we can get someone to go in your place. I'm sure there're plenty of young Irishmen — " He stopped. As clearly as though she had turned around and seen it, Katie was sure that someone — probably Mrs. Lacey — had shaken her head at him. James the footman was not Irish. No one at the table was. The only Irish person in the room was herself. A hot anger rose in her. As she handed a plate to James her hand shook.

"Keep it steady," he whispered.

She wanted to throw it at him, but managed to restrain herself.

"I'm bound to say," Mrs. Carrington's English voice stood out among the other voices, "that if they are instituting this draft, it doesn't seem just that only the poor — in this case the poor Irish — should be the ones to serve. After all, they didn't create slavery, own slaves or bring them over here."

"No," Mr. Lacey said, a satiric note in his voice. "It was the English colonists who started it all, bringing the wretched negroes over here and selling them."

There was a silence. Katie suddenly found herself remembering something Mrs. Alberts had said to the housemaid when she didn't know Katie was listening: "Sometimes her ladyship's English ways get on Mr. Lacey's nerves."

"Grandmamma," Christopher said. "It's the Union! That's what the President talks about when he makes speeches. It's more important than anything else."

"Pay attention, girl," James said sharply.

For a moment, just a moment, Katie thought about pushing the plate he was holding so everything on it would fall down his spotless front. But, as always, the knowledge of how much her pay went to feeding her family held her back. It's stinking, rotten, unfair, she thought. Why should they have so much and us have so little? Talk about the Ascendency! Silently she put vegetables and some beef on the plate and handed it back to James.

That night after dinner she kept some food back, wrapped this time in newspaper, and again went through the pretense of going out to the back so she could give it to Paddy.

Paddy was waiting at the mews gate for her and she slipped through and sat down on the mounting block so she could watch him gobble up the scraps she brought. And where was Jimmy? she thought. Shouldn't he be taking care of Paddy? She watched Paddy chase after a scrap.

" 'Tis a greedy dog you are," she said lovingly. He really was looking a lot better. Still thin, he wasn't at this point all bones, and he hadn't quite lost his puppy look. His paws were almost as big as the coach dog's down the mews.

It was while she was sitting there that she heard a loud drunken voice that sent a chill through her. It was Carson. He seemed to be coming towards them because his voice was getting louder. Paddy looked up.

"Quick, Paddy," she said. Stooping hurriedly, she wrapped up what food he hadn't eaten, then, picking him up and putting him under her arm, she slipped back through the gate to the house's garden. Holding him in her arms, she stood there for a moment, behind a tree trunk. Then, as though fate were against the two of them, she heard the kitchen door open and Mrs. Alberts's voice. "Katie, are you out there? I'll be locking the kitchen door, so you'd better be getting back."

She had no idea what would happen if she took the little dog up into the kitchen, but she knew exactly what would happen if she let him back out into the mews while that coachman, whose voice was still carrying on, was able to get at him. And Jimmy didn't seem to be anywhere. And if Mrs. Alberts locked the kitchen door, she herself wouldn't be able to get back in.

"Come along, Paddy," Katie said, and went up the steps to the kitchen. When she opened the door, Paddy jumped down into the kitchen.

"What are you doing bringing that creature in here?" Mrs. Alberts said, her voice rising indignantly.

"If I leave him outside, Mrs. Alberts, he's sure to be killed by Carson. He's already kicked him in the sides."

"Well, why not? They don't want stray dogs in the mews eating the food that belongs to the coach dogs. Take him out again this minute."

"I will not," Katie said. "I'll take him when Carson goes in." Somehow, she had to get him to Jimmy's room in the Grenvilles' coachhouse down at the other end of the mews.

"Come here, you!" Mrs. Alberts said, picking up a broom.

"No!" Katie cried, snatching Paddy up in her arms. "No, Mrs. Alberts. I'll take him out."

Mrs. Alberts was still advancing, the broom in her hand, when the door opened and Mrs. Carrington came in.

"Oh," she said, glancing at Katie. "What an appealing little dog. Is he yours?"

Katie dropped a curtsy. "Yes, ma'am." She glanced at the red-faced cook. "I was just taking him out."

"I see." Mrs. Carrington, who was tall and had clear, rather penetrating gray eyes, glanced from the cook to Katie to Paddy. "What is his name?"

"Paddy — ma'am," Katie said, still cradling him. If she could get Paddy out before Mrs. Carrington

38

left, she could get him away from Mrs. Alberts's broom.

"All right," Mrs. Carrington said. She glanced up at Katie's face, then turned to Mrs. Alberts. "My daughter is not feeling too well, Mrs. Alberts. I wondered if I could take her some tea."

"Of course, ma'am," the cook said ingratiatingly. "I'll just see right to it." She turned and barked, "Katie!"

But Katie had slipped out the back door. She knew she'd have to pay later, but she had to get Paddy to safety.

Once outside she crept to the gate. Then she ran over the cobblestones to the Grenville stables. "Jimmy," she said desperately. "Are you there?"

He straightened up from looking at one of the horse's hooves. "Yes. I just got back." He glanced at Paddy. "Shall I take him upstairs?"

"Yes. That awful coachman is in our stable and I don't know whether he saw me or not."

"Give him to me," Jimmy said.

She handed Paddy over to Jimmy, who ran up the steps at the side of the stable, opened the door and put Paddy inside. "He'll be all right," he said to Katie.

She wished that he had some way of locking his room, but it was better than having Paddy running around. "Thanks, Jimmy," she said, and turned back to confront the now enraged (she was sure) Mrs. Alberts.

CHAPTER FOUR

Somewhat to Katie's surprise, Mrs. Carrington was still in the kitchen. Mrs. Alberts was nowhere to be seen.

"Well," Mrs. Carrington said with a smile. "Did you get Paddy ensconced safely?"

"Beg pardon," Katie said stiffly, embarrassed. "I don't know what that word means."

"I see. Forgive me. It means settled securely or . . . or snugly."

"I'm much obliged to you, ma'am," Katie said gruffly, "for helping Paddy when . . . when — " She was about to say when Mrs. Alberts took the broom to him, but Mrs. Carrington was an unknown. And she was one of Them. "When — "

Mrs. Carrington smiled a little. "When Mrs. Alberts was about to sweep him out?"

Katie looked at her doubtfully. "Yes — ma'am."

"So what did you do with him? Or shouldn't I ask?"

"I took him to . . . to somebody who'll give him

a bed." If she said it was Jimmy, the Grenvilles' black groom, Mrs. Carrington might tell her daughter, Mrs. Lacey, and the next thing anybody knew Jimmy might get into trouble. Then what would happen to Paddy?

Mrs. Alberts came in from the pantry carrying a tray on which was a teapot, a cup and a small plate. "Katie," she said, "get a piece of that fruitcake from the larder and put it on the tray here. Hurry up." She turned to Mrs. Carrington. "Mrs. Lacey was telling me how much she liked the cake the other day, ma'am. Or is she feeling too poorly for cake? Would she rather have a bit of bread?"

"No, I think the cake will do very well. Thank you." Mrs. Carrington reached for the tray.

"Katie, you be carrying the tray for Mrs. Carrington."

"Yes, Mrs. Alberts."

Mrs. Carrington opened her mouth as though to say something, then seemed to change her mind. Katie took the tray and followed her from the kitchen.

"Be sure now you come right back, Katie me girl!"

There were times, Katie thought, as she followed Mrs. Carrington through the swing doors to the front part of the house and up the stairs, that Mrs. Alberts almost sounded Irish, as if she had reverted to the land of her birth.

When they got to Mrs. Lacey's bedroom, Mrs.

Carrington opened the door for Katie. Holding the tray carefully, Katie walked slowly over the thick Persian carpet to the bed.

Mrs. Lacey was in her big four-poster, reclining on several pillows, her fair hair falling over her shoulders, a white ruffled wrapper around her. She was looking pale and unhappy.

"Your tea, ma'am," Katie said, leaning over and placing the tray carefully on Mrs. Lacey's lap.

Mrs. Lacey stared at the tray. "Mother, I told you I didn't want anything to eat."

"I know you did, Anne dear, but I still thought I'd try and tempt you. You ate hardly any dinner."

"I'm not hungry."

She sounded a little like Sean when he was being cross and didn't want to do what she wanted him to.

"You can take this away," Mrs. Lacey said suddenly, holding out the plate with the cake on it.

Mrs. Carrington leaned over and took the plate. "All right. Do you want your tea?"

"I suppose so." Mrs. Lacey looked at Katie. "You may go now."

"Yes, ma'am." Katie dropped a curtsy and left the room, closing the door behind her. She was in the hallway going towards the stairs when the door opened again and Mrs. Carrington appeared, the plate in her hand. "Why don't you have this yourself, Katie? Or save it and take it home if you think your mother would like it."

"Me ma's dead," Katie said bluntly. She added, "Ma'am." In some families, she thought angrily, women turned down cake. In others they died of starvation. And the woman offering the cake spoke in the accent of those responsible for the starvation.

"Thank you, ma'am," she said coldly. "But Mrs. Alberts would never let me take it home."

"I see," Mrs. Carrington said. "I'm sorry." She paused. "Did she — your mother — die of consumption?"

"Ay. Of the sickness, and because she was starving earlier on before we came over, because of the famine." Katie almost flung the words, and as she did so, remembered Paddy. Would he eat cake? Of course the children would love it. "Thank you, anyway, ma'am," she said grudgingly.

"I'll just come down with you," Mrs. Carrington said. "Perhaps a little of Mrs. Alberts's excellent soup would tempt Mrs. Lacey."

As they entered the kitchen, Mrs. Carrington said, "I'm afraid Mrs. Lacey didn't want the cake, Mrs. Alberts, tempting as I know it is." She paused. "I was wondering if, perhaps, a bowl of that delicious soup we had at dinner would rest better with her."

"Katie," Mrs. Alberts said. "Put some of the soup in a small pan to heat up."

"Yes, Mrs. Alberts," Katie said.

She got a small pan from a shelf near the stove, filled it from the big crock of soup and stood, her back to the rest of the kitchen, gently stirring the

43

soup with a ladle as she had been taught to do by Mrs. Alberts.

When she was finished, the soup was poured into a bowl, placed on a tray along with some bread and Katie instructed to take it upstairs.

"That's all right, Mrs. Alberts. I'll take it up. Thank you so much." And Mrs. Carrington left.

When she'd gone Mrs. Alberts turned to Katie. "If you ever bring that dog in here again, I'll see to it you're fired. This is a clean kitchen. I don't need the likes of that in here." She paused. Katie, her backbone rigid, her closed fists hidden under her apron, stood listening. "Why didn't Mrs. Lacey want the cake?" Mrs. Alberts asked. "She liked it well enough before. What's wrong with her?"

"I'm sure I don't know, Mrs. Alberts."

"Where was she? In the sitting room? In her bedroom?"

"She was sitting up in bed, Mrs. Alberts." Katie bit out the words and kept her teeth together. Any other time, with anyone else, she'd have enjoyed a bit of a gossip. But with Mrs. Alberts —

"How'd she look?"

Katie stared at Mrs. Alberts, taking in the flushed skin and narrowed eyes. There was more here than just the usual eagerness by the staff for any information about the family. What was on Katie's ready tongue was something like, And who am I to be so bold as to make a judgment as to how a fine lady, sitting in her lace and lawn in a four-poster, may feel? But the tense, white look on Mrs. Lacey's face came clearly back to her at this point. "Like there was something really bothering her," she heard herself say.

"Ah. I thought so!" Mrs. Alberts turned away. "Go on to bed now," she said over her shoulder.

"What's goin' on?" Katie asked, despite herself.

"Nothin' that concerns you," Mrs. Alberts said. "Now go to bed."

Next to wishing something lasting and painful would hit the cook, Katie would have liked to know what that immovable woman was talking about.

"You'll still be serving at the table in Bertha's place for the next day or two," Mrs. Alberts said two mornings later. "So be sure your uniform is clean and your hair combed."

"Did Bertha go home?" Katie asked. "She wasn't in her bed last night or this morning." She half expected to be put in her place by the cook. But she had long held that if she didn't ask anything, she'd never learn anything, and a rap or two with a wooden spoon on the hand was a price she found herself willing to pay.

"She's poorly," Mrs. Alberts said abruptly. "Mr. Lacey sent for the doctor who said she was to stay in bed, so she went home where her sister can look after her."

"But will she be all right?" Katie asked anxiously, remembering Ma.

"That's no concern of yours. You mind your work and be sure to pay attention in the dining room tonight. James has told me some stories, me girl."

Master Christopher's guest, Stephen Hedley, was there again, and the talk around the dinner table inevitably went to the war. But to Katie's surprise, Master Christopher said nothing. He sat there, his head down most of the time, his eyes on his plate. Mrs. Lacey was also silent, though she occasionally roused herself to say something, but never about the war.

Since Mr. Lacey was fairly taciturn by nature, the conversation did not flow, and what there was, was carried on by Stephen Hedley and Mrs. Carrington.

"So you're planning to enlist, Stephen," Mrs. Carrington said. She paused a second. "How does your family feel about that?"

"Er . . ." Stephen paused, glanced at Christopher and Mrs. Lacey, then said without much expression, "They're enthusiastic, Mrs. Carrington. My father is an abolitionist and my mother believes strongly in it, too."

Mrs. Lacey spoke for the first time. "And how does she feel about the danger of your being killed or maimed?"

"Mamma!" Christopher said. "The chances of that aren't that great — "

"No? I wonder if the parents of those whose bod-

46

ies are buried at Bull Run and Antietam would agree with you."

There was another stiff silence. Then Mrs. Lacey rose. "Excuse me," she said, and went swiftly out of the dining room. She had hardly touched her dinner.

After another moment of silence, Mrs. Carrington also rose. "Excuse me," she said. And she also left.

Mr. Lacey, whose plate was still half full, put down his knife and fork. Christopher had also barely touched his dish. Only Stephen Hedley's plate was almost empty.

Katie watched him with fascination as he collected the last piece of chicken and bits of vegetable in his fork and put it in his mouth. He was the one going to war, she thought, and it didn't seem to bother him at all.

"I think — " Mr. Lacey began.

But at that moment Mrs. Carrington came back into the dining room. "Anne is a little overtired and needs to rest. Perhaps I can take some soup up to her later." She picked up her knife and fork, glanced swiftly around the table, and then put them down again, as though finished.

Her son-in-law glanced at her. "Entirely finished, Mamma?" he said, and murmured, "Don't let u hurry you." But it was obvious that his mind somewhere else.

"Yes, it was delicious, but I've had quite

Katie, putting the dishes James handed to her on the tray, was pretty sure Mrs. Carrington was not being entirely truthful. She just didn't want to keep the others waiting.

"Is Anne all right?" Mr. Lacey asked abruptly.

"Oh yes. Just a little . . . strained, perhaps."

"She's upset about my enlisting," Christopher blurted out. "But even if I don't enlist, I'll probably be conscripted. I'm twenty-two and according to the *Tribune* all men between twenty and thirty-five will be called. When are they drawing the lots?"

Stephen leaned sideways so James could take his plate. "Next Monday. But — " He glanced at Mr. Lacey. "If your family really doesn't want you to go, remember they can pay three hundred dollars so somebody can go in your place."

Christopher turned on him. "And you think I'd do that?" he asked angrily. "I told you. I want to go."

Katie suddenly found herself thinking of what Dorothea had said, about her brother saying he didn't want to go. Christopher had denied it immediately, but Katie wondered if it were true.

"Katie!" James snapped in an undertone. "Pay ____ on!"

____ Stephen is right," Mr. Lacey said. "And
____ ertainly have enough of the — " He
____ e saw him glance at her and then away
____ t her anger rise she thought of Brian,

and thanked God he was only nineteen. Of course, if the war lasted another year he'd be conscripted, but with any luck it would be over.

During dinner in the kitchen the talk was about nothing but the draft — who would be taken, who'd be exempt.

"You've a brother, haven't you?" James asked, finishing up his plate.

"Brian's not yet twenty," she said quickly.

"Pity," James said. "The army needs all it can get. Lee is pushing it hard."

"Then why don't you go?"

"Now listen, me girl," Mrs. Alberts intervened, "you keep a civil tongue in your head. The impudence! James is married and has three children. It's the young unmarried men who should go and do their duty."

"Like Master Christopher," Katie said. She knew she was courting trouble, but she was so angry she didn't care. "Or will they pay to keep him out? Like all the rich Protestants!"

"And what else do the Irish have to do?" James sneered as he stood up and left the table. He himself was English and had been hired in London by Mr. and Mrs. Lacey on one of their trips. "It isn't as though they were good for anything else. Most of them can't even read!"

"How dare you!" Katie shouted and jumped up, for the moment beyond caring what would happen to her. "And why do you think they can't read? It couldn't be because the bloody English took our land and refused to let us have our Catholic schools and when the famine came threw us out onto the roads to starve, could it?"

"What on earth is going on?" Mr. Lacey stood in the doorway of the kitchen.

"I'm very sorry, sir," Mrs. Alberts said, getting up and bobbing a curtsy. She stared angrily at Katie. "But Katie here forgot her manners and was shouting at James."

Katie stared back at Mr. Lacey, her blue eyes blazing. "I'm Irish and I won't hear the Irish being slandered by the English."

"I was about to tell Katie, sir," Mrs. Alberts said, her own face red, "that since she feels that way it isn't proper for her to go on working in an English household."

"But we're not English, Mrs. Alberts," her employer said mildly, "and I don't blame her. I've heard sneering comments about the Yankee doodle do's in London, and I didn't care for it. Besides, aren't you originally Irish yourself?"

Katie, watching, saw Mrs. Alberts's full cheeks go pink and then red.

"That was a long time ago, Mr. Lacey, sir," she said, then added obsequiously, "And I now consider myself lucky to be an American."

"As do I. Still, most of us came from somewhere. The Irish have the misfortune — or, who knows?

perhaps the good fortune — of being the newest arrivals." He glanced at James. "Katie is right not to take any slander from someone who came over on the ship even later." He half turned away, then looked back towards Katie. "Do you have a brother, or brothers, Katie, who might be affected by the draft?"

"Just me brother Brian, sir. But he's not yet twenty."

Mr. Lacey stared at her for a moment. "That must make you feel relieved," he said. He looked over at the footman. "James, I want to speak to you about tomorrow's plans." And Mr. Lacey turned his back and left the kitchen.

James threw down the polishing rag he'd been using on his shoes, flung an angry look at Katie and followed him.

By now enough time had passed for Katie to reflect on what she had done. But she couldn't bring herself to apologize. She stared at the cook, who stared back.

"Get those dishes washed and dried," Mrs. Alberts said angrily. "And then take that garbage out. Here I make a good dinner and most of it comes back! See to it!"

"Yes, Mrs. Alberts." Katie started cleaning off the dishes, careful to keep the uneaten bits of chicken and other edible portions to one side out of Mrs. Alberts's sight. The Laceys' loss of appetite would mean a good dinner for Paddy.

When she'd finished scraping the dishes and putting them in the sink, she said, "I'll just take this bucket out to the bins at the back."

"All right," Mrs. Alberts said. "But don't waste any time. I'm tired and I want to lock up!"

CHAPTER FIVE

❧

It was a hot, stuffy night, and for all that the Laceys' house was cool by comparison with the cramped tenement rooms down at Five Points, it was a relief to be outside.

Going quickly down to the gate, Katie whispered, "Paddy!" and immediately heard the scrabble of paws on the mews cobblestones, accompanied by whines and whimpers.

"Be quiet! You silly dog!" she whispered again, then opened the gate and felt Paddy's enthusiastic body hurling against her. "That's enough now," she said. "That's enough." But, since she was holding him against her and stroking his head, Paddy didn't pay much attention.

In a moment she released him and put down the broken kitchen dish she'd taken from the pantry, emptying into it the pieces of chicken, bread, potatoes, and anything else she thought the hungry dog would like. As she watched Paddy wolf down the food, she remembered that that plate, dropped by Mrs. Alberts herself a few days before, had been put aside by her with the words, "I'll just get James to glue the piece back. And we can use it here in the kitchen." Perhaps she won't remember, Katie thought, and pushed away the reflection that "Waste not, want not" was perhaps the cook's favorite saying.

While Paddy was chasing the last of the food around the plate, Katie emptied the rest of the rubbish into the big metal bins that stood nearby. She knew Mrs. Alberts was waiting to lock up and that she ought to go back inside immediately. But she was tired and hot and decided to rest on the mounting block and cool off for a moment before she had to climb to her hot room under the roof. The angry cook would soon enough yell at her to come in. Her decision to cool off was immediately foiled by Paddy, who flung himself up into her lap.

"Ach now, Paddy," she whispered. "It's no use getting ourselves comfortable." Nevertheless she sat there, Paddy's small form on her lap, her arms around him to keep him from falling.

She was aware that others were in the mews, but didn't pay much attention until she heard a familiar loud male voice, which she recognized as belonging to Carson. She wondered where Jimmy was and if he were in the Grenville stables working, or out with the coach. If so, remembering he'd said there was no lock on his door, she knew that Paddy could easily get out of his room even if she could put him in there, and then he'd run down again to the Lacey stables, looking for her. Even so, he was better off down there than here and perhaps she could devise some way of keeping him there.

"Come along, Paddy," she whispered and got up, still holding him in her arms. "Let's go."

At that moment Mrs. Alberts's voice floated out the back. "Katie. Come back in at once! I want to lock up!"

Katie stood, caught between her fears of what would happen to Paddy if she simply put him down and of being locked out by Mrs. Alberts, who was in no mood to be patient.

Fortunately, at that point she heard another coach enter the mews at the other end and prayed it would be the Grenvilles'. It was. Peering around the stable wall, she saw Jimmy jump down from the perch and go to the horses' heads. Another man, holding the reins, climbed down from the driving seat. "Hurry up, Jimmy," he said, "I don't have all night. Get the horses into the stable and out of their harness."

Then the man who spoke strolled towards the Lacey stable. Katie was hiding on the other side of the stable, clutching Paddy in her arms, one hand around his mouth in case he should decide to bark. The Grenvilles' coachman came into view in the flaring gaslight of the street lamp. Katie, watching him through the crack made by the open stable door, shrank back. She had no idea what kind of man he was. He might be as cruel as Carson. If he passed the Lacey stable he couldn't fail to see her and

Paddy. But luckily he turned into the stable and Katie could hear him greeting Carson.

Crossing to the other side of the mews away from the street lamp, Katie tiptoed over the cobblestones past the open stable door and then sped down to the Grenvilles' stable.

"Jimmy," she whispered. When he came out of the stable, she said, "Can you take Paddy? I'm afraid of that coachman. He might try to hurt Paddy again."

"Probably would," Jimmy said. "You'd better give him to me." He held out his arms and Katie put the wiggling Paddy into them. Paddy gave a little whine.

"Hush now," she said. She looked at Jimmy. "Will he be all right now, or will your coachman kick him, too, when he gets back?"

"I won't give him a chance. I'll take Paddy up to my room now."

"But if you can't lock the door from the outside — "

"I'll put a box in front of it."

Katie patted Paddy's head. "Be a good boy now!" she said, and ran back towards the Lacey house, letting herself through the gate. But when she mounted the few steps to the back door she found it locked.

Fear and anger thrust at her, anger because she knew the bad-tempered cook had done it deliberately, fear because she didn't know what would happen to her if she were locked out.

For a moment she stood frozen. She debated knocking and calling out. But that would bring trouble down on her head for sure. Then, running down the steps, she went to one of the cellar windows and was relieved to find herself able to open it. It was a small window set high in the cellar wall. If she'd been any bigger she wouldn't have been able to get through. But she was small and thin and just managed to wiggle her body through and then drop down onto the cellar floor. Closing the window again, she tiptoed in the dark to the steps leading up to the kitchen door and turned the doorknob, praying that door wouldn't be locked. It wasn't. She breathed a sigh of relief.

"So, you've decided to come back in, have you? And just how did you get into the cellar? By forcing a window, I suppose, just like a common thief!"

"How dare you call me a thief!" Katie cried.

"Only someone who steals would think to come through a window," Mrs. Alberts said.

"You locked me out."

"I lock the door at nine sharp. You're supposed to be in by then."

"I told you — I had to take out the rubbish to the bins."

"Aye, and feed that mongrel, I'm sure. Taking the food from the kitchen to give him!"

"I only gave him the food that had been thrown out. You know that very well."

"I saw you take that plate and slip it into the rubbish. What were you going to do with it? Take it home?"

Katie, who had hidden the plate behind the front of her apron, pulled it out. "You want it back? Here it is. I took it out so the wretched dog would have something to eat on."

"A likely story! You were going to take it home, I'll wager! I — Oh," she said as Mrs. Carrington's tall form appeared in the kitchen doorway. "Sorry, ma'am. Is there something I can do?"

"I came in to get some more soup for my daughter," Mrs. Carrington said, coming further in. She looked from the cook to Katie. "What seems to be the matter?"

"I was just telling Katie, ma'am," Mrs. Alberts said with an angry look at the kitchen maid, "that the back door is shut at nine and she must be back by then."

"But you were accusing her of stealing something, weren't you?" Mrs. Carrington said. "A plate, I think, and food."

"Well, me lady, it's well-known that the Irish who've just come over here are frequently caught stealing — "

"They are not!" Katie shouted at her. "You have no right to say that! I was just giving some of the food in the rubbish to Pa — to the dog."

"If she was just feeding leftover food from the rubbish to the little dog," Mrs. Carrington said, "what harm can it do? And I really don't think accusing a whole race of people as you were doing is quite fair."

"I'm sure I have no wish to be thought unjust," the cook said stiffly. "Katie, please get some soup from the larder and put it in a pan. I'll just get it heated for you, ma'am."

Standing over the pan, stirring the soup, Katie was painfully aware of both the cook and Mrs. Carrington standing there, waiting for her to finish. As soon as the soup was hot, she put it into a small bowl, covered it, and put it on a tray.

"Thank you," Mrs. Carrington said. "Katie, would you please carry it for me to Mrs. Lacey's room?"

When they got upstairs Mrs. Carrington took the tray from her. "Thank you. I'll take it now." She smiled a little. "Were you feeding the little dog I saw in the kitchen the other day?"

Katie stiffened. "Yes, ma'am. But it was food that was being thrown out."

"I'm sure it was. I wasn't accusing you."

Katie swallowed and was horrified to discover she was on the edge of tears. "I don't know why people hate the Irish so much. It isn't as if we did anything to them. It was the English that did it to us. Me da said — " At that point she realized she was talking to someone who was English. "Beg pardon, ma'am. I forgot . . . ." She stopped, embarrassed. No matter how she phrased it, it would sound rude.

Mrs. Carrington smiled. "It doesn't matter. And I agree. The Irish have every reason to hate us. I know. My brother was in Parliament and worked with Sir Robert Peel to try and do something when the blight hit the potato crop. But nowhere near enough was done. You can run along now. I'll leave the soup plate outside the door when Mrs. Lacey's finished."

Katie dropped a curtsy. "Yes, ma'am." She was turning towards the stairs when she remembered that the Englishwoman had stuck up for her. She turned back. "And thank you," she said.

During Katie's next afternoon off the talk at the O'Farrell dinner was of nothing but the draft. The names were to be drawn the following Saturday at the district office on Third Avenue and Forty-sixth Street.

"And you can bet your boots they'll be Irish names," Katie's father said. "I can't see all those Prots — the kind you work for, Katie — letting their sons be taken. They'd pay the three hundred dollars first."

Katie immediately thought about Christopher Lacey. "He did say when they were talking about it at dinner that he wanted to go like his friend. But then, Dorothea, his sister, said the other night that she thought he didn't really want to. And I don't think his mother, Mrs. Lacey, wants him to go. In

60

fact," she went on, as a sudden thought struck her, "I wonder if that's what she's so upset about. Mrs. Carrington came to get soup for her because she went to bed without eating her dinner when the subject came up. It's unfair," she said angrily. "Why should boys like Brian go and get wounded or killed?"

"I'd go," Brian said. "If they'd pay me the three hundred dollars."

"You would not," his father said.

"Yes, I would, Da. It's filthy and awful here. I want to go out West where things are different. Maybe I could work and get a farm, like the one we had back in Ireland."

"Don't be daft," his father said. "You'd not get a farm for three hundred dollars."

"They say the government's offering land to anybody who'll go out to the new territories. That's where I'd like to go. At least I'd get somewhere where I could make more."

"And you might be killed," Katie said. There'd been an older brother who'd died before they left Ireland, and she was especially fond of Brian. "And besides, why should you go and fight for the blacks?" She paused. "It's not us that made them slaves."

"No," her father agreed, "it isn't. And there's no need for us to go and free them. Anyway, if the Union army wins and takes over the South the slaves will all come up here and take away our jobs by

61

working for less. We don't want that happening. You're not of draft age yet, Brian, so stay where you are. With luck the war'll be over in a year."

Katie saw Brian glance at his father and then down at his plate again. Fear touched her. What their father said had always been law — especially since Katie's mother died. But she knew that Brian had a mind of his own.

CHAPTER SIX

It was Miss Sutcliffe who, unknowingly, warned Katie about what the Laceys were thinking of doing.

She came out to the kitchen looking for Josephine and Dorothea, who were there trying to talk Mrs. Alberts out of a bit of cake before tea.

"You know how much we love your cake, Mrs. Alberts," Josephine said. "It's better than any of the cakes we get for tea in other people's houses."

"Go on with you," Mrs. Alberts said, obviously pleased. "You know you're not supposed to have any between meals," she said, then, "Katie, bring me the cake box."

It was amazing, Katie thought, going into the pantry where the cake box was kept, how different the cook's voice sounded when she was talking to a member of the family. Once she'd mentioned it to her father.

"Ach, the likes of your Mrs. Alberts'll always be making up to the rich people who pay them. Pay no attention, Katie, and don't ever be like them. Remember what those people would do to us if they had a chance. And what they already did to us in Ireland!"

To her father, there were two kinds of people: the English and the Irish, the Protestants and the Catholics, them and us. And the only possible relationship was enmity.

"But Da," Katie had once said to him, "that was true in Ireland. But Ma said we came here because things would be different." Remembering her mother, her voice shook a little.

"And are they, Katie me girl? D'ye see the American English treating us Irish any better here than they did in Ireland? They make fun of us, Katie. They call us illiterates! They think we're trash!"

Katie, who'd never actually met any real English — or their descendants — in her life, hadn't believed him until she'd gone to work for the Laceys.

The two girls were munching on the cake when Miss Sutcliffe came in. "Now that's very naughty," she said in her English voice. "I told you, you had to wait until teatime."

"But Mrs. Alberts's cakes are so good, Suttie," Josephine said. "And anyway, Dorothea said she was hungry."

Mrs. Alberts beamed at them. "A bit of cake won't do them any harm."

"Well, no more than a small bit, then," Miss Sutcliffe said. "Or they won't have any appetite for tea."

Mrs. Alberts closed the box firmly and held it out. "Katie," she said sharply. "Put it back in the pantry. And bring the vegetables to be scraped for dinner." Then turning to Josephine, she said, "A little bird told me you'll be having a birthday soon, Miss Josephine. There'll be a fine cake for you then. Fourteen, it'll be, won't it? You'll be a young lady!"

Katie found herself looking at Josephine with a sense of shock. With her gold curls and her childish dresses Josephine seemed far younger than Katie. Yet she was only a few months younger. As though aware of Katie staring at her, Josephine looked back. The two girls, almost the same age, stared at one another from different worlds.

Mrs. Alberts saw them and turned to Katie. "I thought I told you to fetch the vegetables! What are you doing, standing there like a lump, staring at your betters? Get on with it!"

After a frozen moment, Katie took the box back to the pantry and paused, aware that she would give anything to be able to walk out. Anything, that is, except the pay so desperately needed to help feed her brothers and sister.

"Oh there you are," Miss Sutcliffe said, appearing in the pantry doorway. "It is true, isn't it, what James was telling me, that your brother Brian is too young to be conscripted? I was just mentioning it this morning to Mrs. Lacey. She is so anxious that Master Christopher not have to go into the army, but finish his studies so he can go abroad. And I'm sure that three hundred dollars would be a great blessing in your family."

Katie whirled around. "Me brother Brian's life is not for sale for three hundred dollars. Why should he go and maybe get killed because Master Christopher doesn't want to put his precious skin in danger — even though he thinks the Irish should be happy to go fight to free the slaves!"

"How dare you speak to me like that?" Miss Sutcliffe said. "You rude, impudent girl! I have a good mind to tell Mrs. Lacey, and you will lose your job, which you deserve to do."

As Katie opened her mouth she saw Mrs. Lacey come up beside the governess. Katie looked at her and said more quietly, "I'll not have me brother Brian sent to fight, ma'am."

"I should think he'd be glad for the money, Katie," Mrs. Lacey said.

Mrs. Alberts put in, "I'm sorry, ma'am, that Katie feels called on to speak to you that way. I have no wish to have such an ill-mannered girl working in my kitchen."

"But we should try to remember, Mrs. Alberts, that Katie is, I'm sure, as devoted to her brother as any of us are to members of our own family." Mrs. Lacey turned towards Katie. "Katie, I wouldn't be offering this if I knew for a fact that Brian didn't want to go. But I think he should at least be told

66

about it and have the chance to make up his own mind, don't you?"

Katie stared at her for a moment. In the weeks she'd been here, Mrs. Lacey had never spoken to her like this. Usually Mrs. Lacey had little time to waste with the lower servants, and when she did speak to them it was as though from a great height. Before this business of the draft came up, Katie's employer talked in her presence only of the dinners she planned to give and the distinguished guests she hoped to have. Now — she sounded like . . . like I was important enough to talk to, Katie thought with astonishment.

"Where does your brother work now, Katie?" Mrs. Lacey asked, in the same kind voice.

Katie was about to answer automatically, On the docks, when she changed her mind and said, as offhandedly as she could, "He works at different places, ma'am." Her heart was pounding so hard she was afraid they'd be able to hear it. She did not want to give away where he could be found.

"I've heard James say he thought young Brian worked on the docks, ma'am," Mrs. Alberts said, with an angry glance at Katie.

"I see. Well, I shall pass that information on to my husband," Mrs. Lacey said. And then, "I'm sorry that you feel I'm trying to take advantage of him, Katie." She picked up her skirt and started to leave the kitchen, but she stopped at the door. "Mrs.

Alberts, I don't want Katie to be punished in any way for speaking up for her brother. I'm sure Josephine or Dorothea would do the same. Come along, girls, Miss Sutcliffe."

"If it were up to me — " Mrs. Alberts started.

Mrs. Lacey turned. "But it isn't, is it?" Then she followed the others out of the kitchen.

For a moment Katie and the cook stared at one another. Then Mrs. Alberts snapped, "Hurry up with the vegetables."

Katie would have given anything to be able to go home and see if Mr. Lacey had been in touch with Brian, or at least warn her father. She wasn't quite sure how he would react. She was fairly certain he was sympathetic to Brian's wish to go West. On the other hand, he would bitterly resent Brian's being paid to put himself in danger to help the fashionable Christopher Lacey avoid serving. As for Brian himself — he had made his desire clear the last time she'd been home. He wanted to go West even if it meant risking his life.

But the draft, scheduled for the following Saturday with lists to be posted Monday morning, would take place before her next day off.

Since everyone knew her mother was dead, it was no use using that as an excuse to be allowed an extra day. It would have to be her father, and she said a quick prayer that she be forgiven for lying.

"Please, Mrs. Alberts, can I have this afternoon

off? Me da is sick and needs me to look after him."

"And how would you be knowing that, young Katie? You haven't been home."

"I got a note, brought by one of my father's friends."

"And all this time I've been thinking you couldn't read, Katie." Mrs. Alberts's voice was pure honey. "Now that I know you can, you can help me out a bit by writing out that receipt I was going to give to Mrs. Jones for baking the shepherd's pie." She pulled open the drawer of the kitchen table and took out a piece of paper. "If you'd just run over this with me, Katie, we can then get to work on it." Mrs. Alberts's little eyes stared into Katie's.

Although Mrs. O'Farrell had managed, before she died, to teach Katie a little, as Katie took the piece of paper and glanced at it, she knew that little was not enough.

"So what do you want to do, Katie?" Mrs. Alberts said. "When you've stopped lying about getting a note, perhaps you'd be telling me the truth."

Katie closed her eyes and counted to ten. Even if Brian took the three hundred dollars, and shared some of it with Da and the children before he joined up and left, they'd need every penny that Katie made because he'd be gone. This was no time to get herself fired.

Katie swallowed. "I want to go home to tell me da about Master Christopher. He wouldn't want Brian going and getting killed."

"This is no concern of yours, Katie. It's for Mr. Lacey and your brother to talk about. Such nonsense!"

"Please, Mrs. Alberts!"

"No. You can have your day off next Wednesday, that is, if I don't need you. But not until then. Now get on with your work, and since Bertha is still off, that will mean doing some housecleaning, so don't loiter!"

An hour later Katie was running a rag around the furniture and ornaments in Mrs. Carrington's room and weighing in her mind, for the dozenth time, whether being able to warn her father was worth being fired.

And what if Mrs. Lacey wouldn't give her a recommendation and she couldn't find another job? What would happen to the children if she had no pay to bring home and give to Da to buy food with? And what about Paddy?

It seemed wicked even to think about him in the same moment as her brothers and sister, but she couldn't help it. He was so funny and endearing. She'd have to find some money to give Jimmy so he could look out for the dog. The memory of the other Paddy, running, running behind the wagon, suddenly sprang, as clear as a picture, into her mind and she found herself crying. "It's all so unfair," she said aloud, rummaging around in the pockets of her maid's uniform.

"What is?"

Horrified that she was not alone, Katie looked up and saw Mrs. Carrington standing there.

"Here," the regal woman said, taking a folded square of linen from the top drawer of her bureau. "Here's a handkerchief."

"I don't need one, ma'am." She then was humiliated to feel her nose start to run.

"I think you do," Mrs. Carrington said, smiling a little.

Katie took the square of linen and blew and wiped her nose, then her eyes. But her eyes kept on running.

"What is it?" Mrs. Carrington said. "Something at home?"

Katie looked up and, even as she wept, found herself thinking that the older woman had kind eyes, then dismissed it as impossible in anyone of her rank and nationality.

"I have to see me da, ma'am," she said. "But . . . but me next day off isn't until Wednesday, and the drawing for the conscription is going to begin on Saturday. At least, that's what everybody says."

"Yes. Is it about your brother, and the money he . . . he might be offered to go in my grandson's place?"

Katie stared back at her. This woman could probably ruin any chance she had of getting to her father first. But there was no use denying it. "Yes," she said, and added, "ma'am."

"You've spoken to Mrs. Alberts?"

Katie was busy wiping her eyes again and blowing her nose, so all she did was nod and mumble, "Yes'm."

"And she refused, of course," Mrs. Carrington said.

Katie stared at her. "How did you know?" She was too stunned to remember to say ma'am.

"Because I know she was trying to get your job for her niece. Bertha told me that before she got ill." She glanced at Katie. "You did know that, didn't you?"

"Yes, ma'am," Katie said. She was embarrassed and angry at herself, but she couldn't seem to stop crying.

Mrs. Carrington sat down on the bed. "Come," she said, patting the bed beside her. "Come sit down for a moment."

Everything in Katie told her she should refuse. In the words her father would use, Mrs. Carrington was the enemy. But she suddenly found herself unable to do that. Instead, she did sit on the bed and for a moment cried herself out. "Me brother Michael died then me ma. Now, if Brian goes, I'm so afraid he'll die."

"But I take it he won't be conscripted."

"No. Not yet, anyway. He's nineteen. All the talk is that they're taking men from twenty to thirty-five. And Mrs. Lacey wants to give him three hundred dollars to go in Master Christopher's place."

"And what would Brian say to that?"

"Ach, he'd go in a flash. He's got a mind of his own and he doesn't like it here. He wants the money to go out West where there's more room and there's land."

"I see," Mrs. Carrington said. She patted Katie on the shoulder and for a moment Katie almost thought it was her mother. Then she remembered where she was and who Mrs. Carrington was. "I'll just be going to finish — " she started.

"Mamma," Mrs. Lacey said, coming in. Then she stopped in the doorway. "What are you doing up here, Katie?"

Katie raised her head. "Mrs. Alberts sent me up to do some of the housecleaning since Bertha is still sick."

"I see. And where did you get that handkerchief you're holding?"

"I gave it to her, Anne," Mrs. Carrington said.

"Oh."

"I'll wash it and give it back to you tomorrow, ma'am," Katie said, getting up. She dropped a curtsy to both women and ran from the room.

"Now really, Anne," she heard Mrs. Carrington say as she approached the backstairs. She slowed down to listen to the two women. Mrs. Carrington went on. "I didn't bring you up to talk to servants like that!"

"I'm sorry, Mamma, but I know that wretched little kitchen maid would do anything she can to persuade her brother not to accept our offer."

"Can you blame her? What if it were your brother?"

"Well, it is my son, and anyway, it's mostly the Irish who're going to be drafted."

"And that makes it easier for them to see their sons and brothers killed? Really, Anne. You didn't grow up with this attitude. At least you didn't have it when you left home."

"I didn't know the Irish then. We didn't have them where we were in Connecticut. You should know that, you lived there, too. Here in New York — "

"Here in New York we are seeing the results of hundreds of years of English rule over the Irish. We took their land, we tried to stamp out their religion, we reduced them to tenant farmers on their own property, and then threw them off their farms if they failed to pay the extortionate rent. I am English and I'm not proud of that. And I'd like to point out that your husband's forebears also found the English hand heavy and threw it off some ninety years ago."

Katie, still listening by the backstairs, found it hard to believe an Englishwoman would echo so much what her father was always saying. For a brief moment she wondered idly what Patrick O'Farrell would have to say about it.

Then she heard Mrs. Lacey's voice, sullen and rather low. "I don't know anything about the history. I want to keep Christopher from going into the army. He's my son and I have a right to do it."

"Yes, I suppose you do, although I'm bound to say I never heard of such a foolish and stupid exemption."

"Why? According to what the paper says the government and the army desperately need the money."

"So they're getting it by setting class against class. The rich can pay to stay out, the poor have to go. It's a receipt for disaster, Anne."

"That's nonsense, Mamma."

"Is it? We'll see."

As Mrs. Lacey turned into the hallway, Katie fled down the stairs to the kitchen.

CHAPTER SEVEN

❧

From then on Katie sensed that Mrs. Alberts was keeping an even closer eye on her, as though the cook wanted to catch her in something damaging enough so she could force Mrs. Lacey to let her fire Katie.

To take off during the afternoon when the servants were allowed a rest period before they had to begin dinner preparations, would supply Mrs. Alberts with more than enough reason. The servants were supposed to go upstairs to their rooms to rest and then change before they began the evening.

Nevertheless, Katie, who had been deliberately slow about washing up after the midday meal, waited until she knew Mrs. Alberts was upstairs and then slipped out the back door.

She was barely out the gate when she heard the racing of paws and felt Paddy hurl himself against her.

"You're a wicked dog, you are," she said, sitting down on the mounting block and opening up a small bundle of leftover food she'd been able to smuggle out.

Paddy gobbled it all up with enthusiasm, then stood, looking at her, his head to one side, to see if she had any more.

"I'm sorry, Paddy," she said. "That's all I could get. And she'd call me a thief now if she could!"

"Who would?" a voice asked.

Katie looked up to see Jimmy standing there.

"Mrs. Alberts," she said, and added, "the cook."

Jimmy looked at her for a moment, then, indicating Paddy, he grinned. "There's nothing wrong with his appetite."

"Faith and there isn't!" Katie said. "Has he been a good boy?"

"Pretty good. I give him some of the dinner the Grenvilles let me have. He seems to like chicken and beef."

"Aye, he does." Katie looked fondly down on Paddy who, accepting that this was all the food there was for the time being, had come up and jumped in her lap. She looked up at Jimmy and said in a low voice, "Has the coachman there — " she nodded towards the Lacey stable a few feet away " — has he made any trouble about Paddy? Tried to get at him or anything?"

Jimmy shrugged. "He saw him with me in our stable yesterday and said he'd talk to his friend, our coachman, about getting rid of him. Something about unwanted mongrels. I didn't pay much attention."

"Did your coachman agree with him?" Katie asked anxiously.

"No. Not then. He just said he'd look into it and then talked about something else. He's not a bad person — when he isn't drinking."

Katie sighed. "Ours is. Mr. Alberts, the cook's husband, used to be head coachman, but he got another job for a house in Gramercy Park. He wasn't bad. But this one is. I don't know why Carson hates Paddy so much — or any dog. Of course he wouldn't pick on one of the fine hounds or spaniels that the rich people have."

"No, he wouldn't. Not if he valued his skin."

Katie got up. "Thank you again for looking after him." She contemplated for a moment what she was planning to do. "If . . . if anything should happen . . ." She took a breath. "If I should lose my job, you will look after him, won't you?"

"Why should you lose your job — if you don't mind me asking?"

Katie hesitated. She found talking to a black strange, or rather, she found it strange when she thought about it. When she and Jimmy were actually talking it didn't seem stranger than with anyone else.

"Because I'm going now to see if I can find me father down on the docks. Mr. Lacey . . . Master Christopher . . . well," she said, "the Laceys don't want Master Christopher to go into the army, what with this draft coming up. Me brother Brian isn't old enough to be drafted, but they want to offer him the three hundred dollars they're all talking about if he'd go in Master Christopher's place. Me father . . . well, I'm hoping he won't let Brian take the money. There's no reason why he should be killed instead of Master Christopher."

Jimmy didn't say anything for a moment. Katie looked at him. "I suppose you're very sympathetic to the ones that want to go. You being black and all. And because that man who brought you up was killed at Bull Run because he believed in freeing the slaves."

"Yes, I am," Jimmy said. "I offered to go twice since January, but they wouldn't take me because of my leg."

"What happened to it?"

"A runaway horse kicked it. He didn't mean to. He was just not broken yet."

"But you still like horses."

"Sure. They have even less to say about what they're going to do than us."

"But they live in luxury, with good food, pulling grand coaches, and with grooms like you to take care of them."

"Yes, if they're valuable. But you ought to see some of the ones pulling carts down by the docks or dead or dying in the knackers' yards."

Katie had seen them, but somehow hadn't viewed them in the same way she would Paddy, or Tabby or the kitten her father wouldn't let her keep. "Yes," she said, getting up. She glanced down at Paddy. "Go with Jimmy now," she said and patted him on the head.

It was a long walk to the docks, and she couldn't be sure she'd be back by the time Mrs. Alberts started looking for her. And if she wasn't — but she couldn't let herself dwell on that. She had to talk to her father before the Laceys did.

She went as quickly as she could, crossing the elegance of Broadway and going south and east towards Five Points. The contrast between the two neighborhoods was striking. Sometimes it took all she could muster to remind herself that for all the filthy streets and tenements and the enmity of the English Americans, they were better off here than in Ireland, where people toiled on their few square feet of land, always in danger of being turned off without pity if they failed to meet the rent.

She'd not actually been to the docks before, because her father had strictly forbidden her to go. "It's not a place for you or any decent girl, Katie. There're good men there. But there're some rough ones, too. And the girls that are there are not . . . not — just listen to me, Katie, and stay away from the docks or I'll take a strap to you."

It was not a threat that frightened her much, because he had never actually done that, though she'd seen him discipline the boys once or twice. Still, she knew he meant what he said.

The docks were down past Water Street, and Katie could tell she was getting near when she saw the tall masts rising like skeletons above the wretched-looking warehouses and hovels near the waterfront. When she reached Pearl Street she stopped, a little frightened at what she saw. Groups of men had gathered. There was a lot of shouting. One man was standing on a box, yelling above the crowd, making speeches and trying to arouse the others.

"And who do you think the draft is going to hit?" one man shouted to the others crowded around him. "The Irish, that's who they're going to draft! They're so grand they want to free the slaves in the South, but they don't want to do it themselves — oh, no, not those fine rich men. They're going to send *us* to do it!"

Katie suddenly knew why her father had told her to stay away. The men at the edges of the crowd were looking at her, and one or two were nudging those next to them. And the few women who were present were dressed in a way that made their profession obvious.

Katie also realized she didn't know which ship her father might be working on, or where it was. But she was determined not to go back to Washington Square until she'd seen him.

A man broke away from a nearby group and came up to Katie. "And what would you be doing here, m'dear?" His lips parted, showing two broken teeth, and he reached out to clasp her arm.

She snatched it away. "I'm looking for me da. He works on the docks."

Another man strolled up. "What's going on?"

Katie said more loudly, "I'm here looking for me da. He works on the docks."

"And what would his name be?" the second man asked.

"Patrick O'Farrell."

The expressions on the men's faces changed slightly. "And you'd be — "

"Me name is Katie O'Farrell."

"Would you be sister to Brian?"

"Ay."

"He's just down the street there with those men by the carters."

Katie had no desire to see her brother. She knew she couldn't even begin to persuade him to turn Mr. Lacey down.

"I came to see me da," she said firmly.

"He might be in the tavern — the Green Man, over there."

Katie crossed the street. When she got to the tavern door she hesitated. In the hot July weather it was open and she could see that inside the bar was full, and it sounded as though everyone in there was shouting. Suddenly the memory of her mother's

82

voice came back to her. "Katie, don't ever go into a saloon. It's no place for a decent girl or woman." Since she could now hear one or two female voices blended in with the general roar, she supposed that they belonged to women her mother would not have called decent.

Facing her in the doorway was a barricade made of men's backs and shoulders. For a moment she wished she hadn't come. Then she straightened her own back, walked in as far as she could and said, "Please excuse me."

When there was no reply, she repeated it in a louder voice. One of the men turned.

"Well now," he said. "If it isn't as pretty a colleen as has come my way today. And what would you be doing here, m'dear?"

"I'm looking for me da, Patrick O'Farrell."

Just as the faces of the men outside had altered subtly, so did this one's. "Does he know you're here?"

For a moment she thought she might lie, then knew it was no use. "No. But I have to speak to him."

"Patrick!" the man bellowed. "Patrick O'Farrell."

Several men turned around, saw Katie, and grinned.

"Who wants me?" Patrick started to push towards the door, saw Katie, and frowned. "Didn't your ma tell you never to go into a saloon? Begone with ye. And what about your work? Have you lost your job?"

"No, Da," Katie said, hoping desperately it was true. "I haven't. But I have to talk to you about something."

"Something happened to your brothers?"

"No, Da. Please come out here where we can talk."

By this time the voices had quieted down and Katie was intensely and uncomfortably aware that the men in the front half of the saloon were interested in what was going on.

"Is that your daughter, now, Patrick?" a voice from somewhere in the middle said. "She's a pretty Irish colleen, she is."

Patrick pushed to the front of the crowd, the beer glass still in his hand. "And what would you be wanting to see me about, Katie? I hope it's important."

"It is, Da, really. Can we just step outside a minute?"

"All right, but be quick. I was at a meeting about the draft and what we could do about it. The bloody Republicans!"

Katie could tell by his voice and by the flush on his face that this had probably not been his first beer, and she hoped that he'd be inclined to listen sympathetically. She also realized that any help from him she might, or might not, get would be decided by which side won out in the contest between his desire to help his own son take the three hundred dollars, and his hatred of the draft and the Republicans, and of the Union army and the cause it served.

Sending up a short prayer that she be given the right words, Katie said, "Da, Mr. Lacey wants to offer three hundred dollars to Brian to go into the army in Master Christopher's place if he should be in the draft." As she saw the familiar signs on her father's reddened face, she hurried on. "I know if he gets to Brian first, Brian will take the money. You remember what he said at dinner the other Wednesday night."

"The bloody damn rich Protestants, paying for their sons to stay safe while somebody else does their job!"

"Yes, Da. But if Mr. Lacey sees Brian, Brian will say yes. Couldn't you talk him out of it? That's why I came here."

Her father's angry eyes, which had been staring over her shoulder, fastened on her. "And did you get permission from that cook — Mrs. Alberts? Or did you just take off so you'd lose your job? You're not an obedient girl, Katie, and you ought to be!"

When Katie didn't say anything, he said sharply, "Answer me!"

"No, Da. I didn't. Everybody in the kitchen rests between lunch and dinner to get ready for the evening. Mrs. Alberts . . . she'd gone up to her room."

"And how do you think we're going to put food on the table for Sean and the others if you lose your job? And you can count on it, me girl, if that's the reason they kick you out, you'll not get a reference, and without that you won't have a prayer of being hired by a decent family."

"Da, I'll get back right away. I promise, and if I can go soon I'll get back before Mrs. Alberts gets downstairs. But please talk to Brian — "

"Don't you be telling me what to do, Katie O'Farrell! Of all the gall! And you under threat of losing your job. Get on back to the house and hope and pray Mrs. Alberts doesn't know of your coming over here. I hope you stand in good graces with her, me girl. I know you think she's strict, but that's what you want when you're being trained." He paused as Katie didn't reply. "Or have you done something foolish to annoy her? Answer me!"

Katie recognized the tactic and for a second heard in her mind her mother's voice: "You know, Katie, you have to understand about men. When they're not sure what to do, or if what they're doing is right, they make a loud noise talking and telling you where you're wrong . . . ."

It meant now, of course, that her father didn't know what he was going to do about Brian. And to try to persuade him further would only make him angrier and less willing to do what she wanted him to.

"I'll be getting back now, Da." She couldn't stop herself from adding, "Please, please, Da, talk to Brian. He's only nineteen. He doesn't have to go. . . ."

As she walked away, picking her steps along the

cobblestones, she heard his voice: ". . . And I'll not be needing you to tell me how to talk to Brian. . . ."

She knew as soon as she opened the back door that Mrs. Alberts was in the kitchen.

"And just what do you think you've been doing, Katie? Taking out the rubbish again? Stealing food to give to that wretched mongrel and talking to the Grenville groom who's helping you with him? You think I don't know what's going on here?"

Katie stood there, sure now that the worst was about to happen. But before it did, the door into the rest of the house opened and Mrs. Lacey and Mrs. Carrington came in, with Josephine and Dorothea.

"We're going to be out, Mrs. Alberts," Mrs. Lacey said, "so there won't be anyone here for tea." She glanced at Katie and smiled. "I know my husband has sent a messenger down to Brian at the docks, Katie, asking him to come here before dinner so we can talk to him." She hesitated. "We're all hoping so much that he can help out Christopher in finishing his studies. Perhaps when Brian comes he can come out here and visit you." She looked past Katie to the cook. "If Mrs. Alberts doesn't mind, of course."

Katie glanced at Mrs. Alberts and saw the forbidding woman force a smile. "Naturally, we'll all be very glad to see Brian," she said.

Katie, dazed and still a little frightened, saw Mrs. Carrington smile at her as the two women and the girls left. When the door shut she and Mrs. Alberts were left facing one another.

Then the cook said, "Get your apron on, and be quick about it, Katie. There are vegetables to be cleaned and chopped."

Brian knocked on the front door just before Saturday dinner and was let in by James, who showed him into the front parlor. "Who does he think he is," James said when he came back to the kitchen, "coming to the front door?"

"But it's all right if he saves Master Christopher's life by risking his own," Katie said angrily.

"The impudence!" James said angrily. "Mrs. Alberts, did you hear that?"

"There's silver to be cleaned in the back pantry, James," the cook said. "Katie, go and get it and bring it in here."

Katie knew the cook was trying to get rid of her so she could talk to James. But she went to the back pantry, put some of the silverware on a tray, and brought it in. Placing the tray down on the table, she returned to the sink and went on scraping the carrots. She was heartsick because there was no doubt now that if Master Christopher were drafted, Brian was going to take the three hundred dollars and go in his place.

Suddenly there was a pounding on the back door.

"Who could that be?" Mrs. Alberts said. "Who'd make such an unholy noise?"

She went to the back door and opened it. "Now just who — "

But Katie, watching, saw an arm reach out and push her aside, and as the man came into the kitchen, she realized with horror that it was her father.

"Is Brian here?" Patrick asked loudly.

"How dare you?" Mrs. Alberts said, coming forward. "Pushing your way into my kitchen like that. Who are you?"

"Da?" Katie said, her hands in the sink, not believing what she saw. But her father's red face made it all too clear why he was there.

"Answer me question," her father thundered. "Is Brian here?"

"He's talking to Mr. Lacey and Master Christopher now," James said. "And what would you be doing here?"

"Da," Katie said, going towards him.

"Don't interfere, me girl," Patrick said, thrusting her aside. "I'll be going to the front of this grand house to see what's being offered to Brian. I'll not have anyone trying to get him cheap! I know people like this. Out of me way."

"James," Mrs. Alberts said. "Go and tell the master who's here."

"I'll be telling him meself," Patrick said, walking across the kitchen to the stairs leading to the parlor floor.

"Da!" Katie said, and then stopped. She was sure Mrs. Alberts, outraged, would fire her. But there was a possibility that he might get Mr. Lacey so angry that he'd refuse to offer the three hundred dollars to Brian. Losing her job would be a disaster, but not as great a one as having Brian killed.

"The cheek of him!" Mrs. Alberts said, outraged. "James, stop him!"

But Patrick was already going up the stairs, his big hand shaking the wooden bannister. Ignoring Mrs. Alberts, who was still talking, Katie dropped the vegetables and went after him.

"You come back here!" Mrs. Alberts shouted.

But Katie was already halfway up the stairs. In front of the stairs was the door leading to the dining room. To the left were doors leading to the front and back parlors. All three doors were closed.

Patrick paused for a moment, looking at the doors.

"Stop!" James said, coming after them.

Paying no attention, Patrick pushed open the door to the front parlor. Katie, right behind him, saw Mrs. Lacey and Mrs. Carrington, standing by the chimney piece.

"I don't care," Mrs. Lacey was saying. "All I want is for Christopher not to have to go to this dreadful war."

"But it's all right for the sons of the Irish to go and die, is it?" Patrick said loudly.

"Who on earth are you?" Mrs. Lacey said.

"I'm the father of the man you're trying to bribe to get killed in your precious son's place," Patrick said, striding in.

"Mr. O'Farrell," Mrs. Carrington said.

At that moment the sliding door between the front and back parlor opened and Mr. Lacey stood there. "What is going on here?" he said.

Katie saw Master Christopher and Brian standing behind him.

Patrick looked at his son. "You'll not be getting killed in this rich boy's place," he bellowed. "Come along with me, Brian. There are better jobs for you than that. And I'll thank you, Mr. Lacey, to stop getting others to do the fighting that your lot started. If the South wants to keep the slaves, let them. It's no business of ours!"

"Da!" Brian said despairingly. "Don't do this. Don't spoil it."

"I'll not be having you getting killed to save some rich man's precious son. That's not what we came over here for!"

"I want to go out West, Da. Where else would I get the money to go?"

"If this sprig is too cowardly to risk his own skin to free the slaves, then — "

But at that moment Christopher's fist struck Pat-

91

rick in the face. "Don't you dare call me a coward! Now get out — !"

At that moment Brian's fists went up. "You keep your hands off of me da!" he shouted.

"You rotten filthy Irish — " Christopher roared and drew his arm back.

"Stop it! Both of you!" Mr. Lacey thundered. He looked at Brian. "I suggest you take your father out of here at once."

Katie's eyes were on her father. He had staggered back against the wall, stayed there for what seemed like a long time, then slowly sank down to the floor.

"Da!" Katie bent over him, shocked. Christopher was thinner than her father, and Katie couldn't believe that he could knock down Patrick, famous for his fists. But when she got nearer she was overpowered by the smell of beer.

Mr. Lacey addressed Brian, his voice like ice. "Take your father out of here! How dare he come drunk to a house like this! If you don't go at once, I'll get the police."

Brian stared back. "Keep your three hundred dollars," he said.

Katie, kneeling on the floor beside her father, heard a cry come from Mrs. Lacey. "Oh, no, no! Please take the three hundred dollars. Please!"

"Come, my dear," her husband said. "There are plenty of other young men who'll be glad to go." He turned to Brian. "Are you going to get your father out of here, or shall I call the police?"

"Oh, we'll go," Brian said. "Come along, Katie, give me a hand."

They got their father up and were headed towards the front door when Mr. Lacey stood in front of it. "Use the back door," he said.

"They'll never get him down the stairs." Mrs. Carrington's calm voice was a contrast to all the others'. "They'll have to use the door here."

"I'll not have — " He stopped. Then, "I suppose you're right." He looked at Katie and Brian with their father's drooping head between them. "But hurry up! James, open the door!"

As they pulled their father towards the door, Katie heard Mrs. Alberts's voice from behind the others: "It's an outrage coming in that condition to a house like this!"

Katie, torn between rage and humiliation, muttered to herself, "But it's all right to be coming to a house like this to do the young master's fighting for him."

As they were getting Mr. O'Farrell to the front door, he gave a sudden heave. A strange sound came out of his throat. Then he vomited onto the polished floor of the entrance hall.

CHAPTER EIGHT

Katie, trying to clean the cramped two rooms where her father, Brian, the three younger children and now, since the debacle at Washington Square, she herself, all lived, went gloomily over the events of the previous evening: Brian's arrival at Washington Square, followed shortly by her father's, the scene in the parlor and their subsequent and humiliating departure. But not before Mrs. Alberts, who had come up to see what was going on, stepped forward and barred the way to the door. "Ye'll not be leaving, Katie O'Farrell," she said, "before you've cleaned up that mess of your father's. Here. Here's a rag." And she pulled at one of several that had been tucked in her apron and threw it at Katie.

"Get out of the way," Brian had said, trying to hold up his father's heavy body.

"Not before Katie does what she's told, and then gets out herself."

"I'll take care of — " Brian said between his teeth and then stopped as James, his fists bunched, came towards him.

"Get back, James!" Mr. Lacey said loudly.

"I'll clean it up," Katie shouted. "Brian, hold Da!"

"Ye don't have to be doing anything for them, Katie," Brian shouted.

"Yes. Yes. Just wait!"

As quickly as she could she went down on her knees and started mopping up her father's vomit from the floor. No one said anything.

"You've missed some here," Mrs. Alberts said, pointing.

"Hurry up, Katie," Brian said. "I can't hold him forever."

"It's a pity he drinks so much," James said. "But then, the Irish do."

When it was done, Katie handed the filthy rags to Mrs. Alberts.

"Hurry up, Katie," Brian said again. "I don't know how much longer I can hold him."

It had been a long trip down to the Lower East Side, but taking Patrick up the stairs was the hardest part of all. Once he was on the bed that he and Brian shared, Katie left them, closing the rickety door between the two small rooms.

Now, the morning after, she was trying to make the rooms as clean as possible. But her mind kept going back to the fact that she'd have to return to Washington Square to see if Mrs. Lacey would give her a letter of recommendation. It was a dim hope and she knew it. As long as Mrs. Lacey thought

Brian might take her son's place in the draft there was a chance she'd try to keep Katie happy — even force Mrs. Alberts to keep her on. Now —

Pulling the meagre cover over the bed that she shared with the three younger children, Katie acknowledged to herself that almost all hope of a letter of recommendation was gone. But she had to try.

Before she could go, though, she'd have to empty the chamber pots.

As quietly as she could, she opened the door between the two rooms and looked in. Her father, his face much paler than when he'd come to Washington Square the night before, was sleeping on the bed. Exhausted after carrying most of their father's weight on the long journey back, Brian had obviously not tried to change him into his nightclothes. So Patrick's trousers and shirt were wrinkled and stained. His reddish beard was spotted with particles of food. Katie, staring at him, found her anger dissipating. Like most men they knew he would relieve his exhaustion by a beer or two in the tavern — and given how hard life was, who could blame him? But he indulged far less often than many of his friends. Going over to the bed, she looked under and pulled out the chamber pot.

Katie hesitated a moment, sorely tempted to do what many of the other residents of the tenement would do: throw the pot's contents out the window. But her mother had told her not to do it. "Ah Katie, our streets are terrible enough. We don't have to make them worse!"

Leaving the room, Katie went downstairs and outside to the privy. All the time she was going down and then back up the stairs she thought about having to go back to Washington Square to beg Mrs. Lacey to give her a letter of recommendation. Suddenly she found herself thinking of Mrs. Carrington. For a moment she wondered whether Mrs. Carrington might give her such a letter, but dismissed it as impossible.

That afternoon found her on the long walk back.

As she came down the front steps of the tenement she saw groups of neighborhood women standing around talking. As Katie drew near some of them stopped talking. Finally one of them said, "And what are they saying about the draft in the grand house you're working in, Katie?"

"Ach," another said. "They're too busy counting the numbers of Irish who can go in their sons' and husbands' place."

Katie found herself unable to think of anything to say. After a minute she started forward again.

"And what are you doing home?" another one asked. "It's not Wednesday, is it?"

"Or have you lost your job?"

Katie paused, wondering if the word about her father and herself had gotten about already. She knew there wasn't an Irish person in the entire neighborhood who wouldn't sympathize. Yet she found she couldn't say the words, Yes, I lost my job. They just wouldn't come out.

Instead, she murmured, "Sorry," and pushed herself as fast as she could to the end of the street.

All along the way the sidewalks were filled with groups of men, some of them shouting, others talking more quietly — almost like conspirators.

Somehow the way back to Washington Square seemed even longer and muddier than before. Finally she reached the north side of the square and stood in front of the house, wondering if she had the nerve to march up the front steps, the stoup, as she had learned New Yorkers called it, and ask to see Mrs. Lacey.

But she knew she didn't. Sighing, she turned left and walked along the pavement to Fifth Avenue and the opening to the mews. To reach the Laceys' back door she'd have to pass the Grenville stables. As she approached, she wondered if she'd catch sight of Paddy, although if Jimmy were out driving the family around, the chances were that Paddy would be barricaded in Jimmy's room. The next moment Paddy was jumping up and licking her face.

"Oh Paddy," she said, and felt the tears start in her eyes. She put her arms around him. "Now what are you doing here? You should be in Jimmy's room."

"No, he's helping me with the hay," Jimmy said, as he came up. He had abandoned his uniform jacket and was in his shirt sleeves.

Smiling despite herself, Katie rubbed Paddy between his ears and looked up at Jimmy. In some way she couldn't exactly define, he didn't look as happy as he usually did.

"I looked for you last night," he said. "I'd taught Paddy a trick Mr. Lowell's dog used to do and I wanted to show you. We — Paddy and I — waited by the Laceys' gate to show you, but you didn't come out. Paddy was very disappointed. Every time I let him out, if I don't keep an eye on him, he's down at the gate there, looking for you."

Katie was about to give some vague reason when she found herself saying suddenly, "I lost my job last night."

After a minute Jimmy said, "Why?" And then, "Anything to do with the draft and your brother's going in the son's place?"

"Yes," Katie said. "That's what it was. Brian, me brother, came by. Mr. Lacey sent him a note inviting him. But then me da — me father — showed up. He . . . well, he'd been in the pub and . . . and. . . . Anyway, there was a muck up. Master Christopher hit me father. Now I don't have a job." She was astonished at herself for saying all this.

"It's offering this three hundred dollars to somebody else to go that's causing all the trouble," Jimmy said.

"It's not fair that if you're rich you don't have to risk your life," Katie said. "Why did they do anything so stupid?"

"The government and the army need money as well as men," Jimmy said gloomily. "The South's proving a lot harder to beat than they thought."

"That's what one of the guests at dinner the other night said. Are they that good at fighting?"

Jimmy shrugged. "Mr. Grenville said that the way the Southerners live makes them better fighters."

"What do you mean?"

Jimmy said, "Most of them ride and shoot all the time. A lot of them are farmers — cotton farmers — and they live on farms, some of them large, they call plantations. That's why they have slaves. To pick the cotton."

"The Irish are good fighters, too," Katie said. "But only for things they believe in."

Jimmy glanced at her but didn't say anything. Katie felt suddenly uncomfortable. "I know you said you were only four when you came up here," she said after a minute. "But your mother was a slave, wasn't she? What did she say it was like?"

" 'Like death,' she said. 'You don't own yourself. You can't go anywhere, do anything, that the master or mistress doesn't want. They can beat you or starve you, because you belong to them.' And some of the owners did."

"Well, having to work for people like Mrs. Alberts, I don't feel free, and in Ireland, we couldn't do anything because to pay the landlord took everything. We didn't have money, and all the crops, except potatoes, were taken away to England. When the blight came and the potatoes rotted, then they threw us off the land because we couldn't pay them. Me da said at least slaves were fed."

"If he feels that way," Jimmy said angrily, "maybe he ought to go down and offer to be a slave." He turned and limped back into the stable.

Katie stared after him in dismay. She hadn't meant to upset him. There wasn't an Irish man or woman she knew who wouldn't have said the same, which was the cause of the anger she could feel on the streets now. But she felt bad when she thought of what Jimmy had done for Paddy. If it weren't for Jimmy, Paddy would probably be dead. And she needed Jimmy. Who else would look after Paddy now that she was dismissed?

Katie was about to walk after Jimmy when Paddy started pawing at her skirt. She glanced down, pretty sure it meant he was hungry. And, of course, she had no food. And no prospect of getting any.

At that moment two things happened. Carson came out of the Lacey stables, leading a black horse carrying a sidesaddle. Paddy, seeing something interesting happening, ran towards the horse. The coachman, hearing his paws on the cobblestones, turned. "Get back, you cur," he said.

"No!" Katie cried. She ran towards Paddy. At that moment Mrs. Carrington, in her riding skirt, came around the front of the mews from the house.

"Paddy!" Katie cried, and flung herself towards the dog, just managing to pull him out of the way.

Carson raised his whip.

"Put that whip down at once," Mrs. Carrington said.

The coachman turned and said angrily, "That's the mongrel dog kept by the nigger groom from the stables there, me lady. He gets under the horses' feet and could cause a nasty accident."

"That's no reason to beat him, Carson. And if I ever see you — or hear of you — trying to strike him again, I'll speak to Mr. Lacey. He opposes any mistreatment of animals."

The coachman threw aside his whip, looked angrily at Katie and said, "Your horse, ma'am."

But Mrs. Carrington was looking at Katie. "I'm sorry about what happened last night, Katie." She paused. "Are you here for some purpose?"

"I . . . I was hoping Mrs. Lacey would give me a letter of recommendation, so I can get another job." Just putting it into words made it seem hopeless.

"Have you spoken to her?"

"Not yet, ma'am."

Mrs. Carrington stood there for a moment, then nodded at Carson, who bent down, his hands cupped. Mrs. Carrington put her left foot in his hands and he lifted her into the saddle. When she was seated with her right leg over the pommel and her skirt arranged, she said, "Let me talk to her first. Come and see me this afternoon around three."

She started to pull up the rein. "Who is looking after your dog — Paddy isn't it? — when . . . when you're not here?"

"Jimmy is."

"Jimmy?" Mrs. Carrington queried.

"Yes, ma'am. He's a groom for the Grenvilles."

Hearing his name, Jimmy came out, glanced at Katie and then at Mrs. Carrington. "You called me, ma'am?"

"Katie tells me you've helped her with Paddy. I think that's very good of you."

Jimmy nodded. "Thank you, ma'am."

Katie, remembering his anger, said quickly, "And I'm very grateful to you, too, Jimmy." He looked at her, then went back into the Grenville stable without saying anything.

"I think I offended him," Katie said unhappily.

"Oh? How?"

Katie told her about the conversation. ". . . And I was telling him that the English landlords. . . ." Her voice faded again. She glanced quickly up at the woman on the horse.

"Yes," Mrs. Carrington said with a slight smile. "It's a problem. Sometimes it's hard to balance different injustices. Unfortunately, there are always enough to go around." As her horse stamped she said, "All right, Caesar, we're going."

Katie stood back as Mrs. Carrington walked and then trotted Caesar out of the mews. She was wondering where Mrs. Carrington would be going on horseback instead of in a carriage, when she remembered Bertha once telling her that Mrs. Carrington liked riding uptown, north of Greenwich Village, where there was open country. "It's what she's used to in England," Bertha had said.

Picking Paddy up, Katie went into the Grenville stable. Jimmy was sitting on a bench polishing a harness. He didn't look up.

"Here's Paddy, Jimmy," Katie said. "Since that coachman is around, maybe you'd be putting him in your room." When Jimmy didn't immediately reply, she added, "I didn't mean to offend you. I'm sorry."

Jimmy looked up. "You know what the Irish are saying to all the negroes they meet? If the draft goes forward they'll go after us before they go down South to fight for us. Three of them have said that to me, one of them one of the coachmen."

"Carson? The one who tried to kick Paddy?"

"No, another one. But I'd bet he feels the same. They all think the draft is our fault." He put the harness down. "I wish I wasn't lame. I'd go and fight in a minute." As Katie, still holding Paddy, stared, he said, "You can put him down. I'll take care of him."

"Thanks, Jimmy."

It was a hot Sunday afternoon as Katie made her way back to Five Points. The nearer she got the worse the smell got. She reproached herself for thinking it. The rich on Washington Square had running water. They also had indoor toilets. They had servants and grooms to sweep the nearby streets of horse manure and other waste and thrown away food. They also paid people to pick up some of their leftover rubbish. No wonder their neighborhoods smelled better!

"You're far too fancy, Katie me girl," her father had said once, "worrying yourself about smells."

"Maybe it's because she works for all those rich people," Brian had said with a grin.

"It is not!" she denied hotly. But it was, of course. Katie was not looking forward to getting home. Her father might be awake and she didn't know what trouble he'd cause out of his own guilt and anger.

When she got to the top of the tenement and opened the door, she saw him in front of the sink, pouring water from a bucket over his head.

"And where do you think you're coming from, Katie?" he said. "You should be at work."

"Now should I?" she said sarcastically. "After the trouble you caused there last night? After you puked all over and I got fired because of you?"

Her father stared at her, opened his mouth, and then closed it. For a minute he stood up over the sink, shaking his head. Katie wondered if he was remembering anything. Finally he said, "You have to get that job back, Katie. We have to have the money. And jobs like that are not that easy to get."

"I'm to go back this afternoon," Katie said.

"And who told you that?"

"Mrs. Carrington." As her father continued to stare, she went on, "Mrs. Lacey's mother."

"And when did she say that? Last night? I don't remember that."

"Do you remember anything, Da?"

He turned. "And you keep a civil tongue in your head!" he roared. "You go back there and say you'll be pleased to be working with them. I know half a dozen men down at the docks with daughters unable to get work — decent work, that is! You're a young girl. I'll not have you doing what some of the girls — no older than you — are doing. Losing your job like that!"

"*You* lost it for me, Da! If you remember anything at all, you remember that."

Patrick stared at her for a moment. Then, pushing her aside, he said, "Out of me way. I have to get down to the docks."

Katie presented herself at the back door at three.

"Now will you look who's here!" Mrs. Alberts said.

"Mrs. Alberts — " Katie said.

"It seems Mrs. Lacey wants me to take you back, even though your drunken father made a scene here. Why she should be so kind — "

"It was Mrs. Carrington that made her do it,"

James said. "And she left a note for you, Katie. Here it is." He handed her an envelope.

Katie stood looking at it.

"Aren't you going to open it? After she took all that trouble?"

"I don't think our Katie can read," Mrs. Alberts said. "Fancy that now. Do you want me to read it for you?"

Katie slipped the note into her pocket. "I'll read it later," she said. "What is it you want me to be doing, Mrs. Alberts?"

"I want you to be doing what should have been done yesterday, you lazy girl. The bedrooms need cleaning out."

Katie thought about protesting that it was Sunday, and that housework like that was never done on Sunday. But she didn't dare.

"Yes, Mrs. Alberts."

"And be sure you make the beds. What with Bertha still being sick and you not here, nobody's had time to do that. Now get going!"

As she went upstairs Katie reminded herself what some of the girls who had come over on the boat with her had been forced to do. For a moment, just a moment, she wondered if doing that would be worse than being ordered around and insulted the way she was here. Then she reproached herself and reminded herself of what Father Lavin would say.

She was in Mrs. Carrington's room pulling the

sheets and bedclothes up when Mrs. Carrington entered the room.

"Ah, Katie, you're here. Did you get my note?"

Katie dropped a curtsy. "Yes, ma'am. Thank you."

"I asked my daughter to give you another chance, but I don't know how long she will be able to restrain Mrs. Alberts, what with the events of last night and her desire to bring her own niece in. But I think my daughter is still clinging to a hope that she can persuade her husband to hire your brother as a substitute."

Katie closed her lips against the temptation to say anything. If that were the case, then her job here was short-lived, because she was fairly sure that Brian — unless he'd changed since last night — wouldn't consider accepting the Laceys' three hundred dollars. But she couldn't be sure. Three hundred dollars was a fortune — at least it was to anybody earning fifteen cents an hour on the docks. She hadn't seen Brian since she'd closed the door of the bedroom in which he and Da slept. She didn't know what the morning might have done in the way of changing him.

Mrs. Carrington was looking at her. "What did you think of my suggestion?"

Katie stared at her. She hadn't even opened the envelope since she couldn't read well enough to know what Mrs. Carrington had written. But to admit she hadn't opened the envelope and that she couldn't read anyway seemed equally damning prospects. For a minute or two they stared at one another, Katie's hands on the soft linen sheets of the bed. Finally she blurted out, "I can't read."

There was a silence, then Mrs. Carrington said gently, "Do you have the note with you?"

Katie drew it out of her pocket and handed it to her.

Mrs. Carrington took it. "What I said was that while we're waiting to resolve this problem you might try to find another job, or I might try and find one for you among our friends."

Katie felt her eyes fill suddenly with tears. "That would be very kind of you, ma'am." She wondered why this strange Englishwoman was taking this trouble.

Mrs. Carrington opened the envelope and pulled out the piece of paper inside. She glanced at it, then said, "Come here, Katie, I want to show you what each word says."

Katie walked over to her.

"Sit down here on the bed beside me," Mrs. Carrington said.

"Now — " And she read the letter aloud, pointing to each word as she pronounced it.

Some of the lessons her mother had managed to give her came back to Katie as she listened and watched and found that, after Mrs. Carrington had explained what they were, she could recognize some of the smaller words.

"Ah, I remember some of them as me ma used to try and teach me, before she got so sick and weak."

"Did you enjoy learning when she taught you?" Mrs. Carrington asked.

"I did. And I was sorry when the fever got so bad and she couldn't do it."

"Did the doctor explain to you what the fever was?" Mrs. Carrington asked, folding the letter.

"The doctor? A doctor only came once. He came around looking for sick children from that big hospital — the one uptown."

"Bellevue?"

"Yes. That's the one."

"And no other doctor came?"

"No. And we had no way to get her to the hospital."

"They'd have sent a wagon," Mrs. Carrington said. "If you'd sent for them."

"She died suddenly. We weren't thinking. . . . That doctor did use a word, a funny word. I'd heard it before."

"Tuberculosis?"

"Yes. That was it."

Mrs. Carrington got up and busied herself for a moment while Katie finished making the bed. Then Mrs. Carrington said, "Katie, would you like to learn how to read?"

"Ay. I would. But I don't know if . . . well, Mrs. Alberts says I'm slow about me jobs now."

"We'll find the time, somehow." She smiled. "And now I have to change. You'd better get on with the rooms, or Mrs. Alberts will be after me, too."

Katie curtsied. "Thank you, ma'am."

When she was down the hall in Master Christopher's bedroom, she stood for a minute, staring out the window onto Washington Square. Everything was so muddled, she thought suddenly. Especially people. Mrs. Carrington was English, and Jimmy was black. One of them was offering to teach her to read, something no one except her mother had ever done. And Jimmy was looking after Paddy for her. All the voices of caution and anger, telling her whom to trust, whom never to trust, were there, part of her mind. But . . .

After a minute she started making Master Christopher's bed.

CHAPTER NINE

When Katie came down to the kitchen at five-thirty on Monday morning, she learned that the names of the men who had been conscripted had been published in the *Tribune*, and that Christopher Lacey's was among them.

"The master had a young man from his bank wait at the paper and bring it up here," Mrs. Alberts said. "James said Mr. Lacey read the paper and then took it up to the mistress."

"He must have been upset," said Bertha, who was back. She looked, Katie thought, sallow and thin, as though she should have stayed in bed another week, but after another week's absence the Laceys might have hired someone else.

"Ay," Mrs. Alberts said. "But I'll warrant the mistress will be more so."

At that moment the bell rang. Mrs. Alberts glanced up at the row of bells. "It's from the mistress's bedroom."

Bertha put down the dishes she was putting away and left the kitchen.

"Katie," Mrs. Alberts said. "There's a great stack of dishes and pans over there need washing. Don't dawdle!"

In a few minutes Bertha was back. "The mistress . . . she's that upset. The master's with her. He said I was to bring tea up right away. Oh, she was carrying on something dreadful. Crying and saying she'd die if Master Christopher had to go off to the army. That the master had to find someone right away who'd go in his place."

Both women turned and looked at Katie. "You'd think some young man would be glad to go in his place, wouldn't you?" Mrs. Alberts said.

Katie knew she was being baited, but she made up her mind not to respond. Besides, if she answered, she'd be doing the unpleasant cook a favor.

"And, of course, despite all their fine words," Mrs. Alberts went on, "some of these young men just off the boat are so cowardly — "

Katie immediately forgot her resolution. "My brother is not a coward," she shouted.

"You keep a civil tongue in your head," Mrs. Alberts said, "or — "

But at that moment the same bell went again. Before anyone could start upstairs James appeared. "Katie, you're to go to Mrs. Lacey's bedroom at once. She wants to talk to you."

Katie stood for a moment with her hands in the soapy water.

"Well, what are you wasting time for?" James said. "The mistress wants to talk to you right away."

Katie dried her hands on a towel and followed James out the door and up two flights of stairs to the main bedroom floor. Mrs. Lacey's bedroom was the first one she came to. Mr. Lacey's bedroom was in front of his wife's and the rooms were connected by a sliding door. When Katie knocked and went in she saw Mrs. Lacey in bed, her head and shoulders resting on pillows, her face in her hands. Sobs shook her shoulders. Mr. Lacey was standing by the window looking out, his hands clasped behind him. Sitting on the bed beside her daughter was Mrs. Carrington. She looked up when Katie came in. "Good morning, Katie," she said.

Katie dropped a curtsy. "Good morning, ma'am."

Mrs. Lacey lowered her hands, showing her face blotched, her eyes streaming. "I want you to take a note from my husband and me to your brother, Katie. We will give him far more than the prescribed three hundred dollars to go in Christopher's place."

"Anne," Mrs. Carrington said. "Wouldn't it be better to send the note by someone else? You know how Katie herself feels about it. After all, she's as concerned for her brother as you are for your son."

"But her brother wants to go. He said so himself Saturday night when he first arrived."

"And before that — " Mr. Lacey glanced at Katie. "That was before his father arrived. Let me

114

try again at the bank, my dear. I'm sure there are other young men who would be attracted by the idea of all that money."

"But you yourself said that all of those who were draftable, who could afford it, had already found someone else, while those who weren't had already agreed to go for the sons of some of the bank officers. I can't think why you didn't get someone to go for Christopher."

"Because I thought that Christopher — I mean . . . I thought we had the right person in young Brian O'Farrell. How could we know?! . . ." He glanced at Katie and said, "Yes, well . . . I'll be going to the bank now and I'll do my best to find someone."

"But, Katie, please," Mrs. Lacey pleaded, "won't you think of your brother's great desire to go out West and take him this note from us? After all, it's what he wants. And we mustn't be selfish, must we?"

"I'm sure James would take the note, Anne," Mrs. Carrington said. "Why don't I ask him?"

"But Anthony was going to send James with a note to a friend of his who employs a number of Irish men who thought we might find a substitute among them." Suddenly with her hands she struck the quilt. "Oh why don't we let the Confederate states secede if they want to?" Her voice was close to hysteria.

Her husband turned. "The fight is to preserve

the Union, my dear, not just — or even not mostly — to free the slaves. We can't let states secede when they feel like it."

"How can you stand there and calmly talk about politics like that, Anthony, and whether states can or can't secede? I've lost three children — two of them boys. Christopher is the only son I have left. I'm not going to see him go off on some hopeless cause and be slaughtered."

Katie drew in her breath to speak, her caution from downstairs forgotten. But she found her wrist suddenly clasped firmly by Mrs. Carrington. She glanced down and saw the older woman's clear gray eyes on her. Katie closed her mouth.

Mr. Lacey said, almost impatiently, "I'm sure somebody else can be found to take the note."

"Are you, Anthony? Then who?"

"Perhaps one of the grooms. Never mind, my dear, I'll find someone."

"All right," Mrs. Lacey said. She glanced at Katie and said indifferently, "You can go now."

Mrs. Carrington followed Katie out of the bedroom. "Do you think you could find some time this afternoon for a short lesson, Katie?"

The old impulse to reject anything any one of these people had to offer was at the edge of Katie's tongue. Then she saw Mrs. Carrington's eyes on her and realized Mrs. Carrington knew exactly what she was thinking. She said, "Maybe, ma'am, when Mrs. Alberts goes up to rest."

As she was turning away, Mrs. Carrington said, "I know it's hard under these circumstances, but try not to worry too much about your brother. It is his decision, after all."

Katie hesitated, then said without expression, "Yes, ma'am."

Mrs. Alberts looked at her when she came in. "Well, what did Mrs. Lacey want?"

"She wanted to send a note to Brian, Mrs. Alberts, but . . . but Mr. Lacey said he'll find someone else to deliver it."

Mrs. Alberts stared at her for a moment, then said, "You've got all those dishes still to wash. Get on with it."

"You'd think, Bertha," Mrs. Alberts ostentatiously addressed the housemaid, "that anyone would be glad of any chance offered to a member of her family, wouldn't you?" When Bertha didn't reply right away, Mrs. Alberts went on, "Wouldn't you?"

Bertha, who looked even more sallow than she did when she first came in, finally said, "Not if it meant sending them out to be killed."

Mrs. Alberts finally left the kitchen shortly after three. "And be sure all those dishes are done and the vegetables for dinner scrubbed before I get down," she said to Katie.

Katie worked away at the dishes while Bertha sat at the kitchen table with rags and silver polish in front of her and slowly tackled a big water jug and some of the tea silver.

Katie looked at her once or twice. Finally she said, "Are ye all right, Bertha? Ye look a bit pale."

Bertha didn't answer her right away. Then she said, "I'm all right when I can sit down awhile. Working again takes me breath away."

"Is it your lungs, Bertha?" Memories of Ma made her hate to ask the question.

"Ay. So the doctor says."

Katie's heart gave a painful thump. She wanted to cry out, "Then you shouldn't be working. I wish I could do it for you." But Bertha needed the pay as much as she did.

Katie touched her arm. "I'm that sorry, Bertha."

"Yes, luv, I know you are." Bertha said.

Mrs. Carrington was still on Katie's mind, but so also was Brian and the note that was somehow going to be sent to him. I should have offered to carry it, Katie thought, and torn it up on the way without telling them or him. But it was too late to think of that now. She was pretty sure what her father would say — that is, if he hadn't been in the tavern too long: that Brian should make up his own mind. Which was what Mrs. Carrington had said.

Right now, while Mrs. Alberts was upstairs and before anything else, she had to tend to Paddy. "I'll just take some of this rubbish out to the bins," she said.

Bertha nodded but didn't say anything.

Wrapping some leftover food from lunch in a piece of newspaper, Katie slipped out the back door. But before she reached the gate into the mews she heard a shout and then a shrill cry of pain from a dog — it could only be Paddy, she thought, and ran to the gate. That bloody Carson.

Frantic yelping was going on as she burst through the gate. She saw the coachman, gripping a thick stick with a crooked end hitched into Paddy's collar to hold him off, while he beat the dog with a whip.

Katie flung herself at the man and tried with both hands to pull down the arm holding the whip. Out of the corner of her eye she saw Jimmy come running with his lopsided gait.

"You — " A stream of ugly words came out of the coachman's mouth. Still holding on to the stick, he tried to reach his whip around to Katie.

"Get Paddy off the stick, Jimmy," Katie yelled. Then she dug her teeth into the thick arm.

Carson gave a bellow, dropped the stick, turned, and grabbed Katie by the hair and pulled. Katie screamed. Paddy, now loose, went for the coachman's boot.

"What on earth is going on here?" Mrs. Carrington's cool voice demanded. She came through the mews gate. "How dare you beat that dog when I ordered you not to?" she said. "And how dare you abuse our servant that way?"

"The wench bit me, ma'am, saving your presence."

"Good for her. I would have, too, if it had been my dog. Drop that whip at once. I shall report this to Mr. Lacey. And if I ever see you touching anyone, or any dog, especially this one, again, I'll send for the police. Now get back into the stables!"

For a moment the coachman stood his ground, then he flung down the whip and stamped into the stables. Just before he got in he turned towards Jimmy. "You just watch out. We're going to get your lot!"

Katie was standing there, shaking, and holding onto Paddy. "He'll kill Paddy if he can," she said. "I wish I could take him home."

"Why can't you?" Mrs. Carrington asked.

"Because me da . . ." It was hard to admit this. "Because me da doesn't have much time for animals. He'd . . . he'd put him out in the street."

"I see. That does make it difficult. Perhaps I should take him into the house with me, but. . . ." She paused.

"Mrs. Alberts'd be that upset," Katie said.

"Yes, I'm afraid she would be. Which would make my daughter's — er — present strain worse."

"I keep him with me as much as I can," Jimmy said. "But I can't keep him in my room all the time. It's too small and he'd go mad. But I'll try and keep a better eye on him. This happened because the farrier was here and my attention was on the horse he was shoeing."

Katie put down the food for Paddy, who promptly

120

gobbled up everything. When he was finished she rubbed his head and patted him. "Try and be a good boy."

Mrs. Carrington said, "Katie, will you be coming back in soon?"

Then Katie looked up at Jimmy. "Could you take him back with you now?"

Jimmy nodded. "I'm sorry about his getting out. I'll try not to let it happen again." He picked up Paddy, then turned and limped back.

When Katie and Mrs. Carrington got back in they found James in the kitchen. He was talking excitedly to Mrs. Alberts but stopped when they came in.

Mrs. Carrington glanced at Mrs. Alberts's face. "Is something wrong?" she asked.

"There's been trouble uptown, ma'am," James said. "Up by the drafting office on Third Avenue and Forty-sixth Street."

"What kind of trouble?"

"A mob attacked the office, smashing the windows and setting fire to the place."

Mrs. Carrington sighed. "Because of the draft, of course. It's not surprising." She glanced at Mrs. Alberts and then left the kitchen.

"What was she doing down here?" James asked.

"I think she came looking for Katie," Mrs. Alberts said. "Had she been asking you to do something now? Her daughter should tell her you're kept busy here."

Katie did not like to lie — Father Lavin would

be the first to say it was a sin — and she wasn't good at it. But she said now, "I think she had a note she wanted me to take somewhere."

"Well, get to the vegetables, then. There's going to be five extra for dinner. Master Christopher's friend is coming, and there's another two couples, friends of the master and mistress."

James started for the door. "I have to go back to the bank. Mr. Lacey may own the bank, but he can't seem to get any of the young men there to go in Master Christopher's place. You'd think they'd want to please him, wouldn't you?"

"Not if it means getting killed in fighting," Mrs. Alberts said. "Not when they have good jobs and wives. Unlike — " She glanced at Katie, but said no more.

Katie was busy scrubbing the vegetables when she heard the sounds of shouting. She paused for a moment, her hands still.

"What's that noise?" Mrs. Alberts said suddenly.

Bertha was coughing, but she stopped and listened. "I think it's shouting."

"Shall I go out and see?" Katie asked.

"No — " Mrs. Alberts started, then changed her mind. "Yes. Go through the mews. See what's happening. I don't like the sound of it at all. And James's gone to the bank. He'd come here with a note for Mrs. Lacey."

"Is she downstairs?" Bertha asked.

"Ay, she was. But she sent back the lunch we

made for her and went back upstairs again. Said she wasn't hungry. Katie, are you going to go out and see what's happening?"

Katie dropped the knife she'd been using on the vegetables and ran out into the mews. She hoped Paddy would still be in Jimmy's room, and also hoped Carson would be out with the coach or busy with the horses. Remembering the vigor with which she bit his arm, she didn't want to run into him.

But, for the moment, there was no one to be seen in the mews. Katie looked left towards Fifth Avenue and noticed nothing unusual — one or two carriages and people walking. She looked right towards University Place and saw a crowd of men milling around and shouting. At the back of the crowd she recognized Carson and one of the other coachmen she'd seen in the mews. Then, suddenly, as though someone had given an order, the crowd started running north towards Union Square. Because of all the noise, she couldn't distinguish what anyone was shouting and then she heard: "Follow him!"

Running to the end of the mews, she peered out, trying to see what they were chasing. Just before they all veered east she saw the figure of a black man out in front, running as though his life depended on it. For a terrible minute she thought it was Jimmy. Then, because he was running so fleetly, she knew it couldn't be. Jimmy with his lame leg would never be able to outstrip a crowd like that.

CHAPTER TEN

Mrs. Alberts had taken one look at Bertha's face before dinner and told Katie to hold herself in readiness to wait on the table that evening.

"I'd be that grateful," Bertha said, and sat down suddenly.

After a minute she said, "It's strange they're still having people to dinner, seein' as what's going on outside."

"Oh, they just live down the square," James said.

So Katie, in Bertha's cap and apron, helped James carry the dishes up the stairs to the dining room.

The table, with five guests besides the family, looked full. This time Katie tried hard to keep up with James, who was passing the soup dishes around as she handed them to him. She also tried to listen to the conversation.

"They attacked the draft offices on Third Avenue and the one on Broadway."

"And when Kennedy was going uptown on Lexington Avenue to see what was going on they set on him and almost killed him. If he's still alive it's a marvel."

"Kennedy?" one of the ladies said. "I don't know who he is."

"The police superintendent," the man who had spoken told her.

"Good heavens! What savages!"

"Well, what can you expect? They come illiterate and wild from the bogs of — "

"Can we interest you in some more soup?" Mr. Lacey said hastily to the speaker. And Katie, glancing at him, had caught him looking at her. The bogs of Ireland, that was what the man was talking about. Her anger rose.

James glanced around the table. "You can help me take up the soup dishes, Katie," he said.

As Katie picked up the dishes, remembering always to do so from the right side, she looked at the man who was talking about the bogs. With his Anglo-Saxon looks and expensive suit he'd never be taken for an Irishman, she thought resentfully.

"Mamma, Stephen's going off to the army tomorrow," Christopher said.

"That's very praiseworthy of him," Mrs. Lacey said, without expression. "I'm sure he'll make a fine officer."

"I was thinking — " Christopher said, and then encountered a glare from his father.

Mrs. Lacey put down her fork and stared at her plate.

"Christopher's going to finish his studies at Harvard," Mr. Lacey said. "It's all settled."

Mrs. Lacey looked up. "Is it?" she asked quietly. "I wish I could be sure of that."

There was an uncomfortable silence.

"What more have you heard from uptown?" Mr. Lacey asked the man seated down the table from him.

"There's pillaging and looting, and the most recent report — a really sad one — is that the mobs have burned down the Black Orphan Asylum."

The lady seated beside him said, "How absolutely dreadful. They are truly savages and should go back to the bogs! Were any children saved?"

"As a matter of fact, all were. With the possible exception of one little girl. There seems to be some doubt about that."

"I do hope she got out," the other lady said.

Mrs. Carrington, who was seated directly across from Christopher's friend Stephen, and who, Katie noticed, had spoken little, said suddenly, "That's horrible, of course, and it must be stopped now, but it's important to remember, I think, that any group, like the Irish, that feels itself without power will often do wild things — "

"That hardly compares to burning down an orphan asylum," one of the other ladies said.

"No. It doesn't," her husband agreed.

Katie set her lips and went on putting pieces of

roasted chicken onto the plates and handing them to James.

"Speaking as an Englishwoman," Mrs. Carrington said, "I sometimes think of that saying in the Scriptures: Something about 'as ye treat others so will they treat you — or whoever happens to be in their path.' The same lack of mercy we English showed towards the Irish — particularly when they were dying of starvation — they are now showing towards the negroes, who are the only ones who have less power today in New York than the Irish."

"They're thieving, illiterate and unemployable," one of the men burst out.

"Katie, would you go downstairs and bring me a little of the tea I bought the other day?" Mrs. Lacey said. "I believe I gave it to Mrs. Alberts."

Katie put down the plate she was filling, with more emphasis than was absolutely necessary, dropped a hurried curtsy and left.

For a moment she paused at the bottom of the steps leading to the kitchen and tried to calm herself. She was well aware that Mrs. Lacey had sent her down for the tea to get rid of her for the moment. And in the midst of her rage, she was grateful. She also thought of the things Mrs. Carrington had said. Father Farrell of St. Joseph's on Sixth Avenue would have agreed with her, Katie thought now, surprised at herself. He was always preaching to his parishioners about compassion and moderation — especially towards the blacks — which often enraged some of his listeners. Since St. Joseph's, the oldest Catholic parish in New York City, was just west of Washington Square, Katie had attended Mass there on Sunday morning since she'd gone to work for the Laceys.

"And what are you doing down here?" Mrs. Alberts said, appearing in the kitchen door.

"Mrs. Lacey sent me down for some of the tea she brought home the other day. She said she gave it to you, Mrs. Alberts."

"Then why are you just standing here like a lump? I'll get the tea for her and you can take it up. She must be feeling poorly."

Katie followed her into the kitchen. "Where's Bertha?" she asked.

"She went up to bed," Mrs. Alberts said tersely. "She wasn't feeling well."

"I don't think she's over her sickness — whatever it is. I wonder if it's what me ma had," Katie said.

"You're not paid to wonder," Mrs. Alberts replied. "But happen you're right. So you just keep yourself ready to take her place — especially when there are guests, Katie O'Farrell!"

Carrying the tray holding a small pot of tea and a cup, Katie went back upstairs to the dining room. As she entered she heard one of the men saying, ". . . And they're hanging or beating every negro they can lay their hands on — as well as the usual looting and destroying and burning. It's outrageous! And we don't have enough police to stop them."

She stood there thinking of Jimmy, and worrying about the fact that he couldn't run well. Clear in her memory was that wretched coachman's threat: "We'll get your lot!"

James took the tray from her. "You can start picking up the dinner plates," he said. "And be quick."

Beginning automatically with Mrs. Lacey, Katie took the plates, putting them on a large tray. As she leaned over to take Mrs. Carrington's, that lady murmured, "Try not to worry too much, Katie."

"If the Union army wins, and slavery is abolished," one of the men was saying, "then we can get rid of outfits like the Blackbirders."

"And about time!" another man said.

"What on earth are the Blackbirders?" Mrs. Carrington said.

"They run an illicit slave trade," the man said.

"Slave trade? Now, almost forty years after it was outlawed? That's horrifying. You mean they bring them over from Africa?"

"No. Mostly the Caribbean. And there's another branch that rounds up the escaped slaves and sends them back South — "

At that moment through the open window there was the sound of breaking glass, shouting, and running feet. Katie, picking up the dishes, paused for a second. Then there was more breaking glass.

"What on earth is that?" one of the men asked.

"Are they beginning to attack us in our homes?" one of the ladies cried.

"James," Mr. Lacey said. "Please see what's happening. If they're attacking the houses on the Square, then we'd be wise to move to the back." He added, "It'd be safer for the ladies."

James put down the tray of dishes that he was about to take downstairs and went to the front window. There were curtains, of course, but they were pulled back. Anyone from the Square who wanted to could back off and see what was happening in the dining room.

In a few seconds he turned away from the window. "The broken glass comes from a house on Fifth Avenue, sir, around the corner."

"And they're gone?" Mr. Lacey asked.

"Yes, sir. I think they've run to University Place and are headed towards Broadway. God help any shopkeepers that are open at this hour!"

"Why, oh why?" Mrs. Lacey said. "It's all this horrible war!" She suddenly covered her face with her hands, then pushed back her chair and got up. "Excuse me, please." There was the sound of her feet going up the stairs.

"Katie," Mr. Lacey said. "Please go upstairs with Mrs. Lacey and see if you can be of any assistance. We'll manage here with James."

Katie put down the plates she was holding, curtsied, and followed Mrs. Lacey up the stairs to her room.

Mrs. Lacey rounded on her. "What are you doing here, Katie?"

"If you please, ma'am, Mr. Lacey told me to come and see if I could be of any assistance."

"The only way you could be of any assistance would be to take my note to your brother and see if he would go in Christopher's place, and I know — I've been told endlessly — that you are not going to do that because your brother might be killed. Well, my son might be killed. He could die, just like my other two boys!" And Mrs. Lacey sank down on the bed, put her hands over her face, and started to cry. "I can't bear it," she said, and lay back against the pillows.

Katie, standing at the end of the bed, found in herself a confused muddle of feelings. Despite Mrs. Lacey's frequently expressed wish to have Brian go as a replacement for Christopher, Katie couldn't help feeling sorry for the woman sobbing on the bed as she clung to the last of her sons. And she felt guilty for feeling that way.

"Do you want me to help you undress, ma'am?" she asked finally.

After a minute Mrs. Lacey quieted but didn't answer.

"Do you want to undress, ma'am?" Katie asked again.

"I shouldn't," Mrs. Lacey said. "There are still guests downstairs. But I can't go down there again. I can't. And I can't breathe with this corset on. Yes."

Katie held out her hand and helped her sit up and then stand. After Katie unhooked her dress at the back, Mrs. Lacey stepped out of it.

What struck Katie as she was putting the dress in the wardrobe and taking the underskirt and petticoat that were handed to her was how clean the linen looked, far cleaner than any she had seen or worn. Then she thought, among the things money could buy were washerwomen. Katie had to do her own washing, and also the younger children's and her father's and brother's, when she got home.

"Bring me my nightdress and my robe, please. They're in the bathroom," Mrs. Lacey said.

Katie went into the bathroom. There, hanging on the back of the door across from the copper tub, were Mrs. Lacey's robe and gown.

After bringing them out, Katie slipped the gown over Mrs. Lacey's head. Then she reached under the gown and unhooked the bodice and corset, and let them drop to the floor.

Mrs. Lacey stepped away from them. "You can put them on the chair," she said.

While Katie was doing that, Mrs. Lacey said, "I take it Bertha is feeling poorly again."

"Yes, ma'am."

"I do hope she recovers soon." Mrs. Lacey went over to the dressing table and sat down. Katie pulled the pins out of her hair. Long, wheat-colored waves fell across Mrs. Lacey's shoulders. She held out her brush. "Please brush my hair just for a minute or two. I'm too tired for more."

While Katie brought the brush down the long, silky, clean hair, she thought of her mother, whose hair she often brushed after her mother had fallen ill. Every so often, Katie would bring up water in a bucket from the pump at the back of the yard. She'd tip some of the water into a bowl and wash her mother's hair, rubbing out the dirt and grease. Then, if her mother was watching, she'd carry the soiled water back downstairs to the privy. If her mother had gone to sleep after Katie had dried her hair, Katie sometimes succumbed to temptation and pitched the used water out the window into the street below. After all, it was hard to think that anything could make the street filthier.

As Katie brushed Mrs. Lacey's hair, her eye was caught by the framed photographs on the dressing table. There were the faces of two boys, one of whom, aged about twelve, looked very like Christopher, and a girl, perhaps six, who reminded Katie of Josephine.

"Yes," Mrs. Lacey said, following her eyes, "those are the children I lost. The last one who died — " she swallowed " — was Henry. He was twelve. But I can't, I can't lose Christopher, too. Dear God, I can't!"

When Katie had turned the bed down, Mrs. Lacey

got into it. As Katie pulled the covers up around her, Mrs. Lacey said suddenly, "I know how you feel about your brother, Katie, my mother has reminded me often enough. But I wish . . . I wish you would give him my note. At least then he can make up his own mind."

Katie was about to refuse when it suddenly occurred to her how much she wanted to get home to see if the children were all right. She couldn't just stay here on Washington Square without knowing what they were doing. It would be just like Sean, anyway, to join whatever crowd was going around, getting into trouble. And if she went at Mrs. Lacey's request, Mrs. Alberts would be forced to accept it.

"If you'll give me your note, ma'am," she said, "I'll try to get it to Brian." If I lose it on the way, she thought, who's to say I didn't do my best? Anyway, Brian can't read any more than I can. It was something she hadn't wanted to say before to the Laceys.

"Oh Katie, would you? I'll explain to Mrs. Alberts. I promise you, she won't get after you. I have the note here, because Mr. Lacey couldn't find anyone to take it. Please, please, take it. And here's some money." She reached for her purse and pulled from it some coins. "If you have to take a carriage, that should take care of it."

Me, ride in a carriage? Katie thought, and then immediately wondered if Mrs. Alberts would let her take some food for the children. She knew the an-

134

swer to that and debated for a moment about asking Mrs. Lacey to speak to Mrs. Alberts. But caution won out. Mrs. Alberts might, grudgingly, let her, but would make her pay in some other way. She might even insist that James go instead.

"Thank you, ma'am," she said, dropping a final curtsy and leaving the room.

CHAPTER ELEVEN

When Katie finally got to their tenement in Five Points, she found groups of women standing around outside the buildings talking excitedly and Maggie on the street with some other children. There was no sign of either her father or brothers.

"Why aren't you in bed, Maggie?" Katie said automatically.

"Don't be daft," Maggie said. "There's too much going on. Did you know that there've been fights and hangin's all over the street?" She sounded excited.

"All the more reason you should be upstairs." But Katie knew that in her sister's place she wouldn't be in bed, either. "What do you mean, hangings?"

"They're hanging blacks," one of the women nearby said.

"They can't be. That's horrible!"

"Why?" another woman said. "If it wasn't for them there wouldn't be the draft."

"But Katie's right," a third woman said. "It's horrible. It was horrible when they did that to us in Ireland and it's horrible when we do that here."

"We didn't come here to save the blacks," the previous speaker said.

"No, but we oughtn't to be cruel to people. We don't like it when it's done to us."

"Does anyone know where me da or the boys are?" Katie asked. "Are they on the docks?"

"Sure, nobody's on the docks now. Most of them have closed down. They're all in the taverns and on the streets. As for Tim and Sean, they're probably with a lot of the other boys who're following the crowds. Did you know they attacked the *Tribune* offices, and *The Times*?"

"I have to find Brian," Katie said distractedly.

"Is that fancy family you're working for going to pay Brian to go into the army? Your da was talking about it in the Green Man."

"Herself wants to," Katie said.

"And you're going to help her save her precious son from getting killed?"

"I said I'd take Brian a letter."

One of the women gave a crack of laughter. "And who's going to read it to him? You?"

Katie turned on her in anger.

"And what about you? *You'll* offer to read it to him?"

The woman didn't say anything.

"I thought your da said he was going to the house

to stop it," one of the other women said. "My Jim said he was talking about it the other night in the saloon."

Katie didn't say anything. The memory was humiliating and she wanted to forget it. "I have to find Tim and Sean," she repeated. "And Brian." She headed east towards the dock area to see if she could find any of them there. She never located Brian, but she did find Sean and Tim with a group of boys who were running along the streets where some blacks lived and throwing stones at their windows.

Katie managed to get her hand around Sean's collar. "You've no business doing this, Sean me lad," she said. "I want you to be going home now. And you, Timothy!"

But she was too late for Tim, who'd taken off down the street with the other boys.

"Sean," she said now, holding firm to his collar. "Where's Brian?"

"Let me go," seven-year-old Sean yelled. "Ye're hurtin' me, Katie."

"Ach now, Sean, how could I be hurtin' you? I'm not touching you. Just your collar! Now answer me. Where was Brian off to? Did he say?"

"Let go, Katie! Ye're hurtin' me cruel!"

"Then tell me where Brian is and I'll let you go!"

"I can't. I can't. I don't know where he is."

"Ach, let him go, Katie," one of the other boys said. "Brian's probably with the gang. They were going off to the Armory to get some of the guns there."

"The Armory!" Without thinking, Katie relaxed her hold on Sean's collar. He felt it and in the next moment had twisted loose and was off up the street.

"Sean!" Katie cried. "Come back here this minute!" But it was useless and she knew it.

She stood there thinking of her mother and wondering what she would have done. Then Katie sighed and turned back towards the docks. If her mother were alive, Tim, Sean and Maggie would be home in bed, and she, Katie, would not be wandering around the streets looking for Brian. And her father would not be in the taverns, he'd be the one to go looking for his son.

As Katie wandered back and forth, going north and then west to the Bowerie, and then back down towards Five Points and returning to the dock area, she became seriously frightened. She'd lived in this area ever since she and her family had come to New York. It had never been quiet and peaceful like Washington Square, or elegant like Broadway. There were always people teeming around the dirty cobblestones, gathering outside the tenements and saloons, talking, gossiping, arguing, even fighting.

But tonight was different. There was an atmosphere of anger and violence in the groups of boys and young men and even some of the women, pushing, shoving, making speeches, yelling and running down the streets carrying boxes and items they'd taken out of stores. Some of them were carrying torches and were setting fire to piles of rubbish in the middle of the road. Everywhere shops had been pillaged, their doors broken open, their windows shattered, their shelves swept bare, many of them set on fire. And around her on every side there was shouting and threats and promises of what would be done to rich people in their houses further uptown and to the blacks for whose sake the hated draft had been levied.

Finally Katie rounded a corner, stopped, and stood still for a minute, trying to make up her mind what to do. But she didn't stand for long. A group of rioters, yelling and carrying sticks, came racing around the corner and knocked her down. The next thing she knew she was lying on the muddy street.

"Go home, lass," one young man yelled at her as he passed. "You're not safe here."

Katie picked herself up and moved hastily to the side of the road. She wasn't safe anywhere, but at least she could get the wall of a house behind her.

And then, miraculously, as she was standing there, she saw Brian, walking down the street with two other young men.

"Brian!" she yelled as loud as she could above the general shouting and noise. "Brian. I'm here!" She had to yell twice more before something made him look in her direction. "They told me you were at the Armory with the others." She called to him.

"You should know better, Katie. You'll not find me with that lot!"

She took the letter out of her pocket and waved it at him. "I've got a letter for you."

He detached himself from the group and came towards her. "Give it to me."

She handed it to him, but a second later another group ran past, jeering and shouting. One of the group, Michael McKelvey, a good friend of Brian's, grinned and plucked it from Brian's hand. "Ye didn't tell me ye'd learned how to read, Brian me lad," he said. "And is this from the fine young man in Washington Square, Brian, who wants you to fight for the bloody slaves and get killed in his place? I'll show you what you can do with it!" And Michael lowered the torch he was carrying and held the letter into it.

"No!" Brian yelled. But it was too late. The cinders of the letter were floating up into the air.

"Shall we go to Washington Square and burn the place down for you, Brian?" Michael said, and ran on.

For a minute Katie and Brian stood there listening to the shouts and yells around them. Then Katie said, "And do you really want to take the money and go, Brian?"

"Yes. I do. I want to go West, Katie. I want to buy some land and start a farm. I want it more than anything."

"But you might be killed!"

"Ay, I might. But I might not. And if I don't, I'll have the money for the land."

"Well," Katie said finally, "you don't need the letter. I didn't read it. I can't read any more'n you. But Mrs. Lacey gave it to me to give you and it's about going in Master Christopher's place. So you can go there anyway and talk to her and to Mr. Lacey and to Master Christopher."

"So you think they've . . . well, they'll overlook what happened?"

"I think she'd overlook anything to keep her son from going."

After a minute he said, "This isn't your day off. Did she send you special with the letter?"

"Yes. And I'd better be getting back. It's only because Mrs. Lacey sent me special that Mrs. Alberts let me go. I wanted to send Tim and Sean home. I saw them here awhile ago. Then they ran off with the McDermott boys and some of their gang. I found Maggie outside the house and told her she ought to be in bed. But I doubt she went. Have you seen Da?"

"He's in the tavern."

Part of Katie longed not to go back to Washington Square. But she couldn't stop thinking about Jimmy and Paddy and what might happen to them. "I'd better be getting back," she said.

"I'll be taking you back to Washington Square," Brian said.

They started to pick their way back, trying to

142

avoid the streets where the most trouble seemed to be happening. But trouble was everywhere. Groups of men and women, shouting and swearing, passed, throwing stones in the shop windows and then kicking in doors and going in to loot. Katie recognized one of the women as coming from Five Points. "Molly!" she cried.

Molly turned and grinned, showing a gap in her teeth. "Come with us, Katie. It's fun! And look at what we're getting!" She held out a gold chain.

"She has to go back to work," Brian said, keeping a firm hold on Katie's arm and pulling her forward. "Come on," he muttered. "They're out for blood and there's no use in getting 'em angry." Moving along the narrow streets, he walked her around the looters or waited until they were inside or finished and gone.

But at one sight Katie gave a cry and stopped. "Oh, no, no!" she whispered. Hanging by the neck from a lamp post, his head dangling forward and his body still swaying, was a black man. In the flickering light of the lamp she could see his eyes were open and bulging and his bloodied face monstrously swollen.

Katie started to run towards him, but Brian held her back. "There's nothing you can do for him now," he said.

"But he could still be alive."

"No, Katie, he isn't," Brian said sadly.

"How do you know?"

"Because . . . because he's not the first like that I've seen."

"But why . . . why? It's so cruel!" Katie cried.

"It's because the people are angry. This is why we have to move West." He took her arm. "Let's go, Katie, I have to get you back!" And he dragged her away.

Finally they crossed Broadway just below the Square and walked up the east side of the Square to the mews.

"Can you get into the back from here?" Brian said.

Katie, her mind still on the horror of what she'd seen, didn't answer for a moment. Brian shook her arm. "Katie!" he said. "Wake up! Will you be all right?"

"Ay," she said finally. "I'll go around the back and into the kitchen." She looked at him. "Do you want to come in now and talk to the Laceys?"

Brian glanced down at his muddy shirt and filthy trousers. "I'd better clean meself up a bit, first."

In Katie's private opinion Mrs. Lacey would be so happy he'd come she wouldn't care how much mud Brian had on him. But that might not be true of Mr. Lacey.

"All right. Now. . . . Take care. Don't get into any trouble, Brian."

"Yes, well, that's easier said than done."

Katie waited until Brian had gone off, then crept

down the mews to the Grenville stables. All she could think about was that man, hanging. But the stable doors were locked fast, with all lights out. Katie sent up a quick prayer to St. Francis that Jimmy and Paddy were safely locked upstairs above the stable loft.

It was late and there was no one in the kitchen when Katie, wondering if Mrs. Alberts had locked her out, pushed open the back door.

Then Mrs. Alberts appeared from the pantry. "So you're back. The mistress was asking about you." When Katie didn't say anything, Mrs. Alberts said, "Well, is your brother going to do what Mrs. Lacey wants?"

Katie took a breath. "I don't know. I think he wants to. But he was too mucky to come to see her tonight."

"What they're doing out there is a disgrace! James went out for a bit and said the Irish are looting shops and then burning them and hanging blacks. They ought to be ashamed! All right, Katie O'Farrell, I can see you pokering up your spine, but I don't see how anyone could say different."

Katie said nothing.

Mrs. Alberts turned away, saying, "You'd better be off to bed now."

Katie wondered for a moment if she should stay up a while longer in case Brian should return that evening. Then knew she was too tired. "All right," she said, and started up the back steps.

* * *

Bertha was already asleep in her cot across the attic room they shared. Katie was so exhausted she went to sleep the moment her head hit the pillow. But her sleep was filled with bad dreams. Once she woke up with a cry when she thought something was dangling over her head. But in the faint moonlight coming through the attic window she saw there was nothing there and realized it was a nightmare. She woke up again at five-thirty the next morning, quickly washed and got downstairs. She wanted to ask right away if Brian had come the night before, but knew that if she revealed her concern that much, both Mrs. Alberts and James would take particular pleasure in withholding the information. So she waited until she was helping Bertha with the breakfast trays for Mrs. Lacey and Mrs. Carrington.

"Do you know if me brother Brian came to see Mr. Lacey and Master Christopher last night?" she whispered to the housemaid.

Bertha glanced quickly around and then whispered back, "I don't think so. I went to bed before you came home. I was that done in! But I'd have heard some talk this morning if he had, I think."

"Be quick there, you two," Mrs. Alberts said. "Katie, you should have finished your tray by now!"

"She was helping me with mine, Mrs. Alberts," Bertha said.

Mrs. Alberts merely grunted, but Katie could feel the surly cook had not taken her eyes from her.

"It's a shame the Irish are such drunkards," James said. "They'll never be anything in this country — not the way they run around fighting and stealing and killing. Who'd employ them?"

"Don't answer," Bertha whispered quickly.

Katie knew she was right and was grateful. At the same time she was fighting herself not to lose control. "Why?" she whispered to Bertha. "Why are they talking like that now?"

"Just shut up and hang on," Bertha said. "I'll tell you another time."

"What are you whispering about when you should be getting that tray finished, Katie O'Farrell?" Mrs. Alberts said.

"She's just making sure she has everything on the tray, Mrs. Alberts," Bertha said. And with the hand nearest Katie, she reached over to Katie's wrist and grasped it. "Say a prayer for patience," she whispered.

So Katie occupied her mind by reciting silently ten Hail Marys and one Our Father. By that time the trays were done.

"Katie, you're to help Bertha take the trays up. Get moving!"

She mounted the stairs to the first floor behind Bertha. As they reached the top and walked around to climb to the second flight, Katie glanced into the dining room where Mr. Lacey, his son and his son's guest were all sitting behind parts of the newspapers, reading and sipping coffee.

When they got onto the second floor Bertha stopped. "You go into Mrs. Lacey's room with your tray, Katie," she said in a low voice. "I know she wants to talk to you."

"She didn't ring for me this morning," Katie said, a little surprised.

"She rang for Mrs. Alberts before you got down and told her that when her breakfast tray was prepared she wanted you to bring it up. Why else do you think Mrs. Alberts would have sent you? She'd have sent James up with me instead."

Katie realized immediately that this was true. She had, in fact, been a little surprised when she was sent up with the tray, but she assumed it was because James was busy.

"All right," she said, and went to the front and knocked on Mrs. Lacey's door.

"Come in," Mrs. Lacey called and then, as soon as Katie came in, said, "Did you see your brother yesterday?"

"Yes, ma'am." Katie carried the tray carefully over to the bed where Mrs. Lacey was sitting up against the pillows, her face white and drawn.

"Well, what did he say?"

Katie put the tray down on Mrs. Lacey's lap, then stood up and dropped a curtsy. She hated what she knew she had to say, but she said it. "He said . . . he said he was still interested in going in Master Christopher's place, ma'am." She stood there, unable for the moment to push herself beyond that.

Mrs. Lacey closed her eyes. "Thank God," she said. Then, as Katie dropped another curtsy and turned to go out, "When will he come here to see Mr. Lacey and Christopher, so they can go together to the drafting office?"

Katie turned. "I don't know, ma'am. He said he would have come last night, but he had to clean some of the muck from the streets off himself."

Mrs. Lacey put her head back against the pillows and closed her eyes and said, "I wouldn't have minded any amount of dirt just so I knew my Christopher wouldn't have to go. Oh, good morning, Mamma," she said as Mrs. Carrington came in.

"Good morning, Anne darling," Mrs. Carrington said. She bent over to kiss her daughter. "How are you this morning?"

"Better. Much better, now that Katie delivered my letter and tells me her brother is still interested in going in Christopher's place. He'll be safe!"

And Brian could be dead, Katie thought. The words were like a knife pointing at her own heart. She had felt many things in the days since it was known that a drafted young man could buy his way out of serving in the Union army by paying someone else three hundred dollars to go in his place: anger, fear, scorn, rage. But the combination washed over her now, devastating and condemning her, because she had helped bring it all about. As she stood and stared at Mrs. Lacey in her relief and pleasure, Katie felt her eyes fill.

Mrs. Carrington got up swiftly and went to Katie, her hand out. "Katie — " she said.

"No! No!" Katie cried, pushing her hand away and running out of the room.

CHAPTER TWELVE

❦

Katie concentrated on washing the breakfast dishes while she waited: waited to be called back upstairs and scolded and made to apologize; waited for Mrs. Alberts to be summoned by the master or mistress only to return to the kitchen and dismiss Katie without a reference for her rudeness to Mrs. Carrington; waited for the master and mistress — or possibly both — to come to the kitchen and themselves dismiss her in disgrace.

When she had run out of Mrs. Lacey's bedroom and downstairs, Mrs. Alberts had taken one look at her tear-streaked face and said belligerently, "Well, what happened?"

But Katie had simply shaken her head and picked up her rag to wash the dishes, which she had proceeded to do through a curtain of tears streaming down her cheeks. From time to time she had put up her arm and wiped her face against her sleeve, but the tears had not stopped. Bertha had taken one look at her, glanced at Mrs. Alberts, then come over to help her until stopped by the cook.

"Katie can do that," Mrs. Alberts said. "There's silver needing to be polished before tonight."

"I'll just be a minute," Bertha said with great bravery.

"It's all right," Katie whispered to her. Truth to tell, she was glad to have something over which she could hide her face. She hated anyone seeing her cry. Often, when she'd been in trouble with Mrs. Alberts, she'd taken pleasure and consolation in imagining herself pouring the soapy wash water over the cook's stringy, sparse hair. But this morning she couldn't even do that. Dismissal was only a matter of time. To be favored by Mrs. Lacey as she had been because she'd helped in finding a substitute for her son in the army wouldn't, Katie was sure, hold up when it came to pushing away Mrs. Carrington's hand, extended only in an act of kindness. Even as she struck the hand, Katie was sorry, because she knew that that was what it was — an act of kindness. But after feeling within her the savage thrust of guilt for helping sacrifice her own brother, the kindness from such an elevated height was more than her stubborn pride could take.

Now it was only a matter of time — possibly moments — until she was dismissed in shame.

And what would happen to Paddy? Or Jimmy, if some of those mobs she'd seen found him? Later in the morning she'd found time to sneak out and run to the Grenville stable to look for Jimmy and Paddy. But there was no sign of them and she had to run back quickly, before she could go up to Jimmy's room. Since then the memory of the night before, of the man hanging from the lamp post, seemed always there, whether she was thinking about it or not.

She glanced quickly to the rubbish pile and with relief saw that it was overflowing the bin in the kitchen. Hurrying, she finished the dishes. Glancing up to see where the cook was, she guessed that Mrs. Alberts had stepped into the pantry. And James was nowhere around. As quickly as she could, she dumped the rubbish into some open newspaper sheets on the floor, then fled out the back just as Mrs. Alberts came back into the kitchen.

Running down the back towards the mews, she heard Mrs. Alberts's voice calling out to her, but she pretended she hadn't heard and went through the gate at the back and looked both ways.

The men standing together in the Lacey stable didn't see her. Their backs were mostly to her and their heads were bent as they talked in low voices to one another. There was something about the way they were standing and whispering that frightened Katie. She stood there, partly hidden by the stable door, holding the newspaper-wrapped rubbish, intensely aware that Mrs. Alberts was liable to come up behind her at any moment. The stench of the rubbish held in her arms and next to her chest made her feel sick.

But her mind was on something else: Where were

Jimmy and Paddy? Had something happened to them already? Putting most of the rubbish in the bin, she made a small bundle of some of the fresher food from the table and ran across and down to the Grenville stables. As she ran in front of the men, still bent over and talking, they stopped talking, raised their heads and stared at her. Ignoring them, she sped on until she arrived at the stables. The coach and horses were gone, and there was no sign of Jimmy or Paddy.

After hesitating for a moment, she climbed the rickety steps to Jimmy's room on top and knocked on the door.

"Who is it?" Jimmy asked.

"Katie." She hesitated. "Are you all right, Jimmy?"

"So far."

"And Paddy?"

She heard Jimmy's halting gait behind the door, and it was opened. A small shape flung itself at her and almost knocked her off the step.

"There now, Paddy," she said, stroking his tan coat as Paddy's tongue frantically licked her cheeks. "Are ye being a good dog?" She started going back down the steps, meaning to feed Paddy the food when she got to the bottom, but Jimmy stopped her.

"I wouldn't do that," he said. "The men are talking about — I don't think they'd have much mercy on Paddy if they found him."

Katie stared up at him. The horror of the night before was vivid. "Jimmy, last night I saw" — she couldn't finish. "I'm frightened for you," she said. "Aren't you frightened?"

He paused. "Yes. But what's the use of that?"

"Couldn't you go somewhere it's safe?"

"Where would I be safe? It's going on all over the city. And how'd I get there? They hanged a friend of my cousin's on Sullivan Street, just south of here. Caught him coming out of the store where he worked and strung him up. Just like that."

"I'm sorry," Katie said after a minute. "On the way from Five Points, last night, I saw . . . I saw a man . . . hanging. It was horrible. I'm so sorry."

"Yeah," Jimmy said. "So am I."

"Here," Katie said, thrusting the bundle of food at him. "This is for Paddy. Or," she added, a little embarrassed, "for you. Do you have enough to eat?"

"I'm not hungry."

"Where are the Grenvilles? Couldn't they help you?"

"They're in the country. They have a house up there. And Mr. Grenville's with them."

Katie leaned down and patted Paddy, who was busy sniffing her boots. "Go back up with Jimmy, Paddy," she said. Lifting him, she handed him to Jimmy. "I'll try and get some more," she said.

"All right. Thanks," Jimmy said. He pulled Paddy in and closed the door.

Brian arrived at the house that afternoon.

"It's your brother," Mrs. Alberts said, looking up through the narrow window grill into the street.

Katie started to leave the kitchen to run upstairs.

"Where do you think you're going?" Mrs. Alberts said. "James'll answer the door."

Katie had hoped to do it herself and make one more plea to Brian not to offer himself for the money. But she could already hear James opening the door. In a minute he came down. "The mistress wants you to come upstairs while they're talking to your brother," he said sullenly.

Katie started towards the door, wondering why they should want her to be there.

"Take off your apron first," Mrs. Alberts said.

Katie hastily untied the belt of the big over-apron she sometimes wore over her regular apron when she was washing the floor — which she had been doing. Then she went upstairs.

Mrs. Carrington was also in the front parlor where Mr. and Mrs. Lacey, Master Christopher and Brian were standing.

Mrs. Lacey glanced quickly at her. "My mother — all of us — thought you ought to be here when we talk to your brother so you will know that we are treating him fairly and according to the law." She glanced quickly at her mother as she spoke.

Mrs. Carrington, who was taller than her daughter, was standing a little back of the others. "Come here,

Katie," she said. "I know how you feel about this."

Brian grinned at her. "Ach, Katie. It's all right. It's like I told you. I can go West and get a farm."

Katie stared at him a long minute. "If you don't get killed first," she said finally. But she knew she couldn't stop him, and shouldn't even try. Of all the family, Brian disliked leaving Ireland the most. Not because the previous years hadn't been bitter, but because he had loved the land itself. Standing there in the Lacey parlor, with all of them looking at her, she tried to think what her mother would have wanted, and could almost hear her mother's voice saying, as she had once or twice in the past, "Ah Katie, you can't dictate fate, no matter how hard you try."

"Then what's the use of the novenas and the Hail Marys if fate's set, no matter what?" Katie had protested.

Her mother, who was in bed with the first onset of her illness, stared past her out the window. "I don't know, Katie. But I know that God works with our prayers, although often not in the way we thought we wanted." She'd turned her head and looked directly at Katie. "So go on saying them, love, for yourself, for me, for the family. God will answer, in His own time and way."

Katie swallowed now. "You have to do what's right for you, Brian. Ma would have wanted it."

Brian left the others and came over and kissed her cheek. "That's a good sister, Katie. I'll be all right. I promise. And when I get that farm, I'll send for you."

"How?" Katie said, without thinking and with some bitterness. "You can't write and I can't read. I'll be going back downstairs now," she said and left the room.

So far those in the Washington Square house hadn't heard too much noise. But that evening, with the windows open in the July heat, sounds of shouting and gunshots and sudden roars as though from a crowd listening to a speech were clearly audible as the family sat down for dinner.

"I wish you'd done what I asked and gone to the country for the month," Mr. Lacey said. "It's not safe even here, now, and the mobs are getting nearer." He glanced around the table. "I want you all to promise me you won't go out for any reason while this terrible riot is going on. Promise me!"

"But Papa," Dorothea said. "Can't we at least go into the Square? We can hardly breathe here in the house. If Christopher goes with us, surely we'd be safe."

"You are not to go, is that clear?" Mr. Lacey glanced down to the other end of the table at his wife. "I want you to be certain that my wishes are observed about this."

Mrs. Lacey nodded. "Of course, dear. The girls will not put a foot outside while this horrible, monstrous riot is going on. When I think of all those dreadful Irish out there — "

"One of whom is going to make sure your own son will be safe no matter what the development of the war," Mrs. Carrington said clearly. "I think that should be kept in mind at all times."

Katie, once again taking the ailing Bertha's place, felt, rather than saw, Mrs. Lacey glance quickly at her.

"Of course," the latter said quietly. "I didn't mean . . ." she murmured and said nothing more.

"I wish — " Christopher said suddenly. "I wish I hadn't made that agreement with Brian and he hadn't taken your money, Papa. I feel such a hypocrite! Our family's always been abolitionist and Republican. I don't think it's right that — "

"Oh, please, please, Christopher my darling!" Mrs. Lacey said, her voice close to tears. "Please don't even think such a thing. After all, there are plenty to go and fight for the Union cause. And I would be ill with worry." She put her napkin up to her mouth. "Please — "

"You should have thought of that before, Chris. It's done now," his father said, glaring at his son. "So just accept your good fortune!"

"But — "

"Christopher!" Mr. Lacey said in a voice Katie hadn't heard before.

"Hurry up," James whispered, as she quickly

filled the plates and passed them to him. When she was finished, James said, "Now go down and get the sweet. You'll have to put the separate plates on a tray and bring them up. Mrs. Alberts has made individual servings."

Katie was feeling almost actively ill. She knew she ought not to have been surprised when Mrs. Lacey, forgetting her presence as she did so often, spoke of the kind of people now in the streets rioting and her pleasure in the fact that her son was no longer in danger of losing his life on the battlefield. It was obvious to Katie that, with her mission accomplished to get her son excused from the draft, Mrs. Lacey, unlike her mother, was oblivious of Katie's feelings and anxieties. Katie had been in the Lacey household for a while now, but never had she seen so clearly that, for people like her mistress, other people who were different, like her own family, were not even human, did not exist.

"The main thing," Mrs. Lacey was saying now, "is that Christopher will be safe," and she glanced lovingly at her son, who kept his eyes on his plate and said nothing.

"What are you dawdling for?" James whispered angrily. "They'll be ready for the sweet in a minute."

Katie went quickly downstairs, and then, as she reached the bottom, suddenly put a hand out to the balustrade to steady herself. It was still light outside, and light came through some of the windows. But it was almost as though she couldn't see.

"What are you doing out here?" Mrs. Alberts said, coming out of the kitchen as Katie clung to the bannister.

"Nothing," Katie said, unwilling to admit to her momentary weakness. "I came to get the sweet."

"Well, you won't find it out here."

Katie followed the cook back into the kitchen. A big tray was on the kitchen table and on the tray were little plates, each carrying a little cake topped with whipped cream. Katie picked up the big tray by its sides.

"And when you come back, you can take this rubbish out to the back," the cook said.

"It might not be safe out there," Bertha said. She was sitting beside the big table, her drawn face pale, almost yellowish in the fading daylight. "James said there were crowds running on the avenue outside the mews, yelling and threatening anything and any-one, and talking about what they were going to do to people in houses like this one."

"They won't hurt Katie," Mrs. Alberts said. "She's one of them and they'll know it the minute they spot her. Hurry now and take the sweets up-stairs. Don't take all day."

It seemed to Katie as she slowly climbed back up the stairs, trying to balance a tray as wide as the staircase, that she would never reach the top. Once, unable to hold on to the bannister, she misjudged the height of the step up and almost fell forward. Then she felt Bertha's hands on her back and side, holding her to keep from falling.

"Steady now," Bertha whispered.

Katie didn't say anything, but paused a minute on a step halfway up. "I'll be all right, Bertha," she said. "But thanks."

James's voice came from above, "Why are you taking so long?"

"The tray's as big as she is," Bertha said.

"That's no reason — "

"It's all right," Katie said. "I can manage." In her present mood she didn't even want help from Bertha. Reaching the parlor floor, Katie took the tray into the dining room and put it on the side table.

"Take these and serve them," James whispered, "starting with Mrs. Lacey."

When everyone at the table was served James said indifferently, "You can go down now."

It was an hour or so later, after the washing up, that the sounds coming through the open windows from Fifth Avenue, the Square and University Place grew louder and more menacing.

"They'll be getting nearer," James said. "Carson told me they'd burned shops on Broadway and Lafayette Street and in the west part of Greenwich Village. The two lots'll close in on us." He glanced at Katie. "A lot of savages they are. It's a good thing they're being drafted."

A part of Katie's mind was fully aware that the footman was deliberately baiting her. With the arrangement between Brian and Master Christopher almost completed, Mrs. Alberts would have no compunction in trying to get rid of her so that her niece could have the job.

But Katie was beyond caring. Part of her took angry pleasure in the knowledge of the fire and destruction created outside by her own people — those who would have to go and finish the war that genteel folk like the Laceys believed should be fought for the principle of emancipation, but of course didn't want their sons fighting. But nagging at her were thoughts about Jimmy. The memory of the hanging man clawed at her. What would happen to Jimmy?

As for Paddy, she knew most people, including her father, would consider her fondness for the stray mongrel puppy ridiculous. Her mother would have understood. For a minute Katie thought about Tabby, whom she'd never been able to find after her mother's death, and who had probably died either of starvation or between a dog's teeth. . . . What would happen to Paddy if a crowd . . . if Carson got hold of him?

"I'll just take out the rubbish, Mrs. Alberts," Katie said.

The cook looked at her for a moment out of her small eyes. "Ay. And ye'd better come back right away. I'll be locking up."

Katie emptied the bin onto open newspaper sheets on the floor. Glancing up to see if she was being watched, she slid some of the fresher food onto a separate sheet, quickly folded it up and hid it behind the bin. Then she bundled the rest up and got to her feet. As she left by the door through the garden, she could feel the cook's little eyes on her back.

"I'll be locking up soon," Mrs. Alberts called after her. "I'll not wait. Not with that lot out there."

"I'll only be a minute," Katie said. And knew she was lying.

CHAPTER THIRTEEN

It was dark now, but Katie could easily see the figures down at the end of the mews, their shadows jumping around in the light of the torches they were carrying.

Katie paused and stared, feeling frightened. At a moment like this, it was suddenly hard to remember that these were her people and that she sympathized with their anger and resentment. Amid the shouts and yells, some words rose clear: "Burn them! Hang them!"

There was no one in the mews. All the stable doors were shut. But Katie was sure the people in the mob could tear them open in a minute if they wanted. They were carrying crowbars and pikes. And then what would they do?

Katie turned and ran as swiftly as she could towards the Grenville stables at the opposite end of the mews. From the shouts from Fifth Avenue she knew that more rioters were approaching from that side. When she reached the Grenville stables she pulled at the door, which opened easily. There was only one horse in the stable. But that wouldn't deceive anyone who knew the stables, and she had no doubt that Carson would be around to tell them about Jimmy in his room above the loft.

Lifting her skirt, she ran up the steps. "Jimmy!" she whispered through the door, and then more loudly, "Jimmy!"

For a moment she thought he might have gone away, and was relieved, only hoping that he would have taken Paddy with him. But when she pushed the door open, she saw him sitting on his bed, his arms around Paddy. Then she saw his face — it was swollen with bruises and covered with blood.

"Jimmy!" she whispered, horrified.

"Have you brought the crowd with you?"

"Of course not," she said angrily. "Why would I do that?"

"You're Irish, aren't you?"

"Yes, but — but I'm not a hangman, Jimmy. What did they do to you?"

"Caught me when I was coming back from seeing my cousin south of the square on MacDougal Street. I got away — thanks to some police who came running, but I managed to punch a couple before I did."

"Why did you go out with the rioters all around?"

"My cousin's old and his wife's not well. I wanted to tell them to get out of town. I knew where they could get a buggy."

"Did they go?"

"No. It was too late. So I started to come back."

"Why didn't you just keep going?"

"Where to? It was too late for me to go, too. Besides, Dobbin's still here."

"Dobbin? The horse in the stable?"

"Yes. He's mine. Mr. Lowell left him to me, and the Grenvilles let me keep him here. The crowd promised to come looking for me. Somebody — Carson, maybe — told them where I stay. So they'll burn the stable and kill Dobbin and Paddy. And me," he added bitterly.

Suddenly, what her fellow Irish were doing came much closer. A sense of horror crept over her again. She stood frozen for a minute. And then the idea that had been in the back of her mind all along became something that had to be done now. At once! "Come with me, quick, Jimmy! I'm going to hide you and Paddy."

"Where?" he said, bewildered.

"There's a cellar below the kitchen in the Laceys' house. I've been down there. I can squeeze through the window and you can, too. Come on. Have you got the rope for Paddy?"

Suddenly he was beside her and Paddy was trying to climb her leg. "Hurry," she said. "They're at the end of the mews!"

When they were on the ground, she said, "Let me look," and went to the door.

The crowd in University Place was still at the end of the mews, and still angry.

"Come to the other side," she whispered, and

ran across the cobblestones of the mews. Jimmy followed immediately, carrying Paddy. Then as quickly as she could she sped back to the Laceys' garden and back gate, with Jimmy and Paddy right behind her. Opening the gate she held it for Jimmy, then ran across the small garden to the window she'd crawled through before. "Quick," she said. "Get in. It's a drop to the floor, but you can manage that."

She stood beside the window as Jimmy first handed her Paddy, then slid through the window and down onto the cellar floor. "Give me Paddy," he said, "and you come in."

She handed Paddy carefully through the window. "Hold his muzzle," she whispered. "They mustn't hear him bark."

When Paddy was safely in, she slid through herself.

It was dark in the cellar, lit only with the flickering light from the lamp beside the Lacey stable. "I'll bring you and Paddy some food," she said. "And a blanket to lie on."

"And some water, please," Jimmy whispered. "I'm thirsty."

Katie nodded. "I'm going to have to go back out the window and then to the outside kitchen door, that is, if Mrs. Alberts hasn't already locked it. She mustn't see me coming from the inside cellar door. Lift me up, Jimmy."

So Jimmy lifted her until she was able to slide out

of the bottom of the window. Straightening her skirt, she slipped around to the staircase leading to the back door and went up, fully expecting the door to be locked.

But Mrs. Alberts was there, drinking some tea. "Took your time, didn't you?"

"I went to the privy at the back."

"Well, go up now. I'm not having you in the kitchen with some of your friends and cousins ready to destroy everything outside they can, and then wanting to come in and loot everything here."

Katie took a breath. "Yes, Mrs. Alberts." She took off the big apron and hung it on the hook behind the door. "Good night," she said and went quickly up the stairs.

She didn't undress but lay on her bed in the darkness, waiting for Mrs. Alberts's feet on the stairs, on her way to the room at the opposite end of the top floor. The room in between was James's. Next to her lay Bertha.

"Are you awake, Bertha?" she whispered.

"Yes." Bertha whispered back. Then, "Why aren't you getting undressed?"

Katie had known from the moment the idea had entered her mind that she'd have to trust Bertha. She also knew it would place a burden on Bertha, and that if Mrs. Lacey found out, they'd both lose their jobs. Whether Mrs. Alberts wanted to get rid of Bertha as much as she did Katie, Katie doubted.

Bertha was Irish, but she was Protestant and north Irish, and anyway, it was Katie's job, not Bertha's, that Mrs. Alberts wanted for her niece.

"I brought Jimmy and Paddy into the cellar," Katie said, knowing she was risking their lives and her own.

"Jimmy and Paddy?" Bertha whispered. "Is Paddy the dog Cook told me about, that you're feeding?"

"Yes, and Jimmy's the groom in the Grenville stables that's helped me look after him. He's black, Bertha, and they're hanging blacks. I saw one. It was horrible! And they've *beaten* Jimmy. His face is swollen and bloody."

"I heard they were doing that — hanging blacks. It must have been dreadful." Bertha was silent for a minute, then, "I won't tell, Katie. But Cook'll have you out quick as a wink if she finds out. Or James will."

"Yes. I know. I have to go down when they're asleep and give them a blanket to lie on and some food and water."

"You're a brave lass, Katie, ye really are."

Katie didn't feel brave. She felt frightened.

After a few minutes she heard steps she was pretty sure were Mrs. Alberts's coming up the stairs. They paused outside the makeshift door that divided the attic into three spaces.

Under the door was a faint, flickering light, undoubtedly from Mrs. Alberts's candle. Lying there,

Katie held her breath, afraid that Mrs. Alberts would open the door to check on her, wishing she had pulled up the threadbare blanket at the end of the cot to hide the fact that she was fully dressed. But if she moved now the cot would squeak, and she was afraid that that would bring the cook in.

But after a few seconds the steps moved away to the front of the attic. The light disappeared and Katie heard the faint sounds of Mrs. Alberts getting undressed and the protesting squeaks from her bed as she settled down in it.

"Has James come up?" she whispered to Bertha.

"No. He went out. He has a key to the back door, you know."

Katie'd forgotten that. But she couldn't let it stop her now.

She waited what seemed like a long time. Then she slowly sat up, and when her bed squeaked, she waited again, to make sure Mrs. Alberts, suspicious, wouldn't come along to see what she was doing, though getting out of bed could mean no more than using the chamber pot or the bowl and pitcher to cool herself with a little water.

But there was no sound from the other side of the attic, so, carrying her boots and with the thin, narrow blanket from her bed over her arm, Katie opened their door as quietly as she could, waited again, then in the dark, her hand on the bannister and feeling her way, she crept down the stairs to the floor where Miss Dorothea and Miss Josephine slept in one room, Mrs. Carrington in another, and Master Christopher in the third. Praying that they were all asleep, Katie descended to the main bedroom floor where Mr. and Mrs. Lacey occupied the front bedroom and Mr. Lacey used his own bedroom back of it as a dressing room. In between was the bathroom where the bath sat with a water pump at the end. This floor and the parlor floors offered the greatest risks because the family, whose adult members arose later in the morning, sat up later at night. The main bedroom and the bathroom doors were closed, but as Katie paused, looking at the cracks under the doors, she noticed that under both doors there was a flickering light, indicating that both the master and the mistress were getting ready for bed.

Katie breathed a little easier as she continued down, then stopped, because on the parlor floor the door of the back parlor was ajar and the candles inside the room still lit. Which meant that Master Christopher was probably inside, reading. Knowing she would have to pass the half-open door, Katie moved with even greater care, not daring to breathe until the door was behind her and she was halfway down to the kitchen floor.

She knew this would be the difficult part, because she didn't dare light a candle in the kitchen. If Master Christopher were indeed in the parlor upstairs, he could, if he passed the open parlor door, see the light from downstairs. Fortunately, there was a lamp outside that partly lit the kitchen.

Creeping into the pantry with a knife from the kitchen, Katie sliced a large wedge from a loaf of bread, put a small wad of butter from the butter dish on top of it, and went back into the kitchen, where she filled one of the jugs with some water and took a small towel from the bottom of a pile of dish towels in a cupboard.

After a moment's thought she put a saucer under the jug. Paddy would need water, too. Then she reached behind the bin to where she had hidden the small newspaper bundle containing some of the meat from the dinner's rubbish before she'd taken the rest out. She was about to wrap all of this — except, of course, for the water jug — in the blanket when she paused. There was something else she needed to take down. Back of the pantry was a small storeroom. Going in there, she lifted as gently as she could a spare chamber pot from under some oddments of furniture and kitchen and gardening utensils. When she got back into the kitchen she added a candle and some matches to her pile. Carrying the blanket-wrapped bundle under her arm and the jug of water and towel in the other hand, she crept down the steps to the cellar door, praying that Jimmy would remember to hold Paddy's muzzle so he wouldn't bark.

Putting down the water jug, she turned the key in the cellar door as gently as she could. Gentle as she was, the key made a noise as the bolt turned, and she waited, hardly daring to breathe, to see if anyone had heard. But apparently no one had. Opening the door, she picked up the jug and towel and stepped through. Then she put the jug down again and gently closed the door behind her. As she did she realized a vengeful Mrs. Alberts, if she suspected — or discovered — where Katie was, could simply lock the door and imprison her in the cellar, along with Jimmy and Paddy. Well, she thought, she couldn't dwell on that now. She picked up the jug again.

"Jimmy, are you here?" she whispered.

"Yes. I'm here."

"Are you holding Paddy's mouth closed?"

"Yes."

Katie crept forward and, after she was away from the door, put the bundle and water jug down and lit the candle she was carrying.

"Hold the candle down," Jimmy whispered. "Those people looking for me could see it from the window."

Katie hastily lowered it and tiptoed over. "Take the candle," she whispered, "while I get the bread, butter, and water."

After she had got those and put them down by Jimmy, she reached over to where Jimmy was holding Paddy and slid her hand around his muzzle just under Jimmy's hand. He removed his hand and Katie sat there for a minute, holding Paddy's muzzle and stroking him. He was trying, unsuccessfully, to lick her, but it was obvious his main attention was on the bundle of food she'd brought.

"Now, don't make a sound," she whispered to him, pulling the bundle over and opening it.

As Paddy gobbled down the food, Jimmy said, "I tried tying the rope around his muzzle, but he hated it and anyway, it didn't work." In a minute or two the food was gone, and Paddy sniffed around the floor for more.

"Himself is hungry," Katie said.

"Here," Jimmy said. He was chewing on the big wedge of bread, but he tore off some and held it out. Paddy sniffed at it.

"You didn't have to do that," Katie whispered. She hadn't dared to bring more in case Mrs. Alberts would notice. She might notice, anyway, of course, but if more were missing, she'd be sure to.

"Oh, I don't know," Jimmy said. He stared down at the bread in his hand. "I'm owing you. But I can't help thinking. Would you be doing this if it wasn't for Paddy?"

Katie was about to answer sharply when the truth of his question hit her. After a minute she said, "I hope so."

He looked up. "I shouldn't've asked that. You could lose your job."

She didn't say anything and for a moment they both were silent, Jimmy sitting with his back to the damp wall and Katie squatting on her knees, both of them watching Paddy chewing at the bread.

Then Katie wet the little towel in the jug and handed it to Jimmy, saying tentatively, "Maybe

175

this'll cool your face and get some of the blood off."

He took the towel, opened it and held it to each side of his face. "That feels good," he said.

Katie noticed that even in the dim candlelight the towel was smeared red. "Are you all right?" she said.

"Fine, now. Thanks."

Katie picked up the blanket she'd brought. "You'd better put this underneath you. It's damp down here."

Leaving the candle and matches along with the other things, Katie crept up the cellar steps and, praying she'd not been discovered, opened the door as quietly as she could.

When she got back up to the parlor floor, the light in the back parlor was out. She didn't know whether this meant Master Christopher had gone upstairs or gone out. She still had to go upstairs herself, which she did, step by step, as quietly as she could. When she passed the doors on the main and children's bedroom floors, she noticed that the narrow strips underneath the doors were all dark.

As she crept into her own cot, Bertha whispered, "Everything all right, Katie?"

"Yes. I think so," Katie said. Something made her ask. "Are you all right?"

"As right as I'll ever be."

"Why do you say that?" Katie asked as she stepped out of her uniform and lay down on the bed.

"I don't know. I just have that feeling."

Katie didn't say anything. She remembered that

her mother once had said something of the same kind, as though she knew what was going to happen to her. And it came over her, as it so often had, how much she missed her mother.

Still thinking of her, Katie whispered, "Say a prayer, Bertha. Perhaps one of the saints will hear you." Then, remembering where Bertha came from and that she was a Protestant, she added, "But you don't believe in saints, do you?"

Katie thought for a minute that Bertha had gone to sleep, but then she heard her say, wearily, "It's all the same God, Katie."

There was something about that remark that made Katie think again about her mother, and then, strangely, about Mrs. Carrington, which, Katie thought as she drifted off to sleep, was very odd.

CHAPTER FOURTEEN

The riots went on. From time to time the noise of the mobs, the shouting, and the cries were louder than at other times, and the tension of those within the house was visible in the strained faces and abrupt voices.

"I don't want any of you to go out," Mr. Lacey said at lunch. "I stayed home from the bank to make sure that you're all going to be safe. But I can't be certain of that unless you stay indoors. Is that clearly understood? No one is to go out."

"But, my dear, how are we going to get some of the food we need? Some of the bread and milk and other necessities?" Mrs. Lacey said. "I was talking to Cook this morning and she said we had less bread than she thought we had."

Katie, standing by the sideboard after bringing up the sweet from the kitchen, glanced quickly at the mistress, wondering if Mrs. Lacey were looking at her as she spoke. But Mrs. Lacey's eyes were on her husband. Mrs. Carrington, Katie noticed, was calmly eating her sweet as though the shouts and yelling from outside were nothing to worry about.

"Don't stand there dreaming," James said impatiently. "Fill the plates."

James, who was inclined to take his cue from Mrs. Alberts, was often impatient, but Katie, her ears strained for any noise from the cellar that couldn't be explained, wondered if he'd heard anything from that region that might have made him suspicious.

"Hurry up!" James said again.

Katie, intensely aware of Jimmy and Paddy two floors below her, was too worried to bother with James's high-handed manner towards her. Exhausted when she'd gone to bed the night before, she'd awakened before five and stolen down to get some more bread and water and hack a little from the carcass of a cooked chicken kept in the coolest part of the pantry.

Jimmy was still asleep on the blanket when she crept down the cellar steps. But Paddy, wide-awake and delighted to see her, had frightened her by barking happily.

"Shush!" she'd said, taking him up in her arms and holding his muzzle closed. "You're not to make a noise like that. You'd be driven right out and so would I."

Jimmy woke up suddenly at the bark. "Sorry. I meant to have my hand around his mouth when you came down. Do you think they heard?"

"I hope not," Katie said. "It's not the family I'm worried about. It's Mrs. Alberts. You know what

179

she's like. But I don't think she's down yet."

"Have you heard anything about the riot?"

"It's quiet now, because it's so early." Then she added despairingly, "If only the police could stop it or do something about it. It's all because the draft is so unfair!"

After that, she took out the chamber pot and emptied it in the privy. When she got back she said, "Jimmy, I wish I could bring you something else to eat, and I will if I can. But Mrs. Alberts, who hates me and wants my job for her niece, watches me all the time, waiting for me to do something so she can fire me."

"It's all right," Jimmy said. "At least I'm not being hanged from a lamp post."

"You're up early," Mrs. Alberts said suspiciously on finding Katie in the kitchen."

"I was in the privy outside," Katie said, relieved that it was true, although not completely.

"I want you to go out to the market near Broadway and get some milk and bread. You're Irish, so they're less likely to attack you than they are me or James."

"All right," Katie said. "Do you want me to go now?"

"No. Breakfast is ready and you have to help James serve that first. Bertha is feeling poorly again."

So she served the breakfast and helped with the washing up, all the time listening for any noise from below.

Her anxiety mounted as the morning wore on. How long could a young black groom and a lively, noisy puppy stay in the cellar without someone knowing?

"You can go to the market now," Mrs. Alberts said after the lunch dishes had been washed. "And try and stay out of trouble. I know they're your friends, but they're killing anybody they meet."

"If that's so, Mrs. Alberts," Bertha said, "then it isn't safer for Katie to go out than any of us, it it? She'd be as much in danger of being killed as we would."

"Of course not, she's Irish like them," Mrs. Alberts said.

"But would they think to stop and ask if she is?" Bertha said.

Mrs. Alberts stared at Bertha for a minute, her lips compressed. "With those blue eyes and black hair they'd hardly miss it!" Then she snapped at Katie, "You'd better go now. Things'll get worse as the day goes on and they start coming out of the saloons."

She went to a grocery shop, passing open, gaping stores with their doors and windows smashed, their contents looted. Fortunately, the one usually used by the Laceys, where she'd bought food for them before, seemed to be more or less intact, which might have been partially due to men standing outside, holding rifles or crowbars. Mrs. Alberts had not given her any cash because the store was used to charging whatever was bought and submitting the bill once a month. She herself had only a few pennies, since she gave almost all her pay to her father to help with the rent and food and had managed to save only a small amount for herself. After she had charged the milk and bread, she used her own pennies to get some biscuits, a little fruit and one or two scraps from the butcher. She was leaving when Carson, who was just entering, bumped into her, knocking the bundle carrying the butcher scraps out of her hand. Before she could retrieve it he had picked it up and was opening it.

"I thought the master always got his meat from the country," Carson said, an ugly look on his face.

Katie, frozen with fear, could think of nothing to say and was standing there when one of the other coachmen came in. "Have you heard, they're bringing in the troops from Gettysburg?" he said to Carson. "That'll put a stop to the bloody Irish and their riots, you'll see."

Carson, momentarily forgetting the meat in his hand, turned to the other man. "Where did you hear that?"

Quick as a flash, Katie took the small package of meat out of Carson's hand and ran out of the store, dodging here and there and managing to get lost among the knots of people before the coachman could find her. But would he come to the kitchen door and ask Mrs. Alberts what the meat was for and make trouble for her? Katie ran towards the mews and through the gate, then veered to the window at the back. Flinging the meat through, she said a prayer that Paddy would have it eaten before anyone knew what she was doing, then slipped quickly to the kitchen door.

Fortunately, Mrs. Alberts was at her afternoon lie-down, and Katie hoped that by the evening the wretched coachman would have forgotten the whole episode.

She went upstairs and washed and changed and returned back down again. Bertha had already changed and was in the kitchen, seeing to the stew-pot on the stove that was gently and slowly simmering the stew planned for dinner.

"Katie," Bertha said quietly. "I heard barking once or twice. I'd have gone down, but I was afraid to leave the kitchen alone in case James or Mrs. Alberts should come down. But I think you'd better go down and see to them. Perhaps some more food — "

But at that moment Mrs. Alberts came down the stairs and into the kitchen.

Glancing at the other two, she went to the hook where James kept the key to the wine and cheese cellar and was taking the key off when, to Katie's horror, there was the unmistakable sound of barking.

"There must be dogs in the mews," Bertha said loudly. "I expect it's one of the Grenville or Stafford hounds."

"And what would he be doing here?" Mrs. Alberts asked. "He'd be kept in the country along with the other hounds."

"I heard he was being brought here for somebody who wanted to buy him," Katie invented desperately.

Mrs. Alberts looked at her with scorn. "And who'd want to buy him in the city here? Don't be daft! And that bark didn't sound like a hound's."

Bertha made a clatter getting out some pots. "Ah well, there're different kinds of hounds," she shouted above the deliberate rattling she was making. "I've heard it said that there are so many kinds even those who know them all have a hard time telling which ones are barking."

"That's a lot of rubbish," Mrs. Alberts said. "Now be quiet." She was standing absolutely still, obviously listening.

Katie prayed that by now Jimmy had his hand around Paddy's muzzle. She knew the cook was watching her, which was perhaps the reason she managed to spill some of the soup she was pouring from a crockery pot into a pan.

"You can just get a rag and clean that off the floor," Mrs. Alberts said. "Of all the clumsy — "

At that moment James came in. Looking at Katie, he said, "Did anybody hear a dog barking a minute ago? The master said it sounded right below our feet and he wanted to know if I'd brought a dog in."

"Or anyone else had," Mrs. Alberts said, staring at Katie.

Katie mopped up the broth, making the procedure as noisy as she dared. But there were no other barks. After a while the kitchen staff seemed to relax and to concentrate on getting the soup, the stew, the vegetables, the salad and the sweet ready for dinner. Muttering something about taking a message from the master to the stables, James went out the kitchen door and headed for the mews.

When he came back a while later he said pointedly to Katie, "I was talking to Carson. He was telling me about the meat you bought. Did you bring it in here?"

Katie froze again.

"What meat?" Mrs. Alberts said. She turned to Katie. "I didn't tell you to get any meat for dinner. Mr. Lacey brings it from the country or James gets it from the market below Houston Street. Why did you get meat?"

"I didn't," Katie said. And hoped she'd be forgiven the lie. "I don't know what Carson's talking about."

"If I find you've been feeding that mongrel with money given you for the food here — "

"You didn't give me money to go shopping with, Mrs. Alberts. You know it's always charged."

"Carson said — " James started.

"Ach, he gets drunk and often doesn't know

185

what he's saying," Bertha said. "It's happened before."

A bell rang from upstairs. James left and Mrs. Alberts said crossly, "We can talk about this later. Katie, get the tray ready with the soup dishes and take them upstairs. James can take up the tureen when dinner's served."

Never had Katie heard an order with more pleasure.

James came back. "Because of the trouble outside Mrs. Lacey said to get the dinner on the table as soon as we could. The later it is, the worse the trouble outside seems to be, I suppose because they all have more time in the pubs."

"Is it true that troops from Gettysburg are coming into the city to stop the riot?" Mrs. Alberts asked James as she emptied the steaming soup into the tureen.

"Ay, the master said something about it and about the police being helpless. The soldiers are due here any time now."

It was during dinner, as Katie was helping James serve the stew, that frantic barking broke out from somewhere downstairs.

There was a silence. "That's the same barking I heard before," Mr. Lacey said. "Is there a dog in this house?"

"Of course not, dear," Mrs. Lacey said. "It must be from the mews."

"I don't think it's from the mews," Mr. Lacey said. "James, did you hear anything before?"

"Not then, sir." He paused and looked at Katie. "Would you like me to go down again and look?"

"Yes. I would."

"Can't it wait until after dinner, dear?" Mrs. Lacey asked.

Katie suddenly found herself looking at Mrs. Carrington, who was looking back at her.

"Get the plates served," James snapped at Katie.

"All right," Mr. Lacey said. "But I want you to go down as soon as we've finished, James."

"Yes, sir," James said, and looked again at Katie.

Katie looked back at him. Then she put down the dish she was holding and turned towards Mr. Lacey. "It's me that has the dog in the cellar, sir. And Jimmy, the groom from the Grenville stables. I was afraid — "

"How dare you, you impudent girl?" James said. He turned to Mr. Lacey. "I'm very sorry, sir, about this. Mrs. Alberts and I both feel — "

"Just a minute, James," Mr. Lacey said. "What were you saying, Katie?"

"I hid them, sir. I saw a black man hanged night before last — " Despite her resolution, her voice shook. "They strung him up and hanged him from a lamp post." Her voice was uncertain for a moment. Then she went on. "I had to help Jimmy, sir. He can't run and they'd have got him. A mob threatened him. And he's helped me with Paddy."

"Who is that?" Mr. Lacey said.

"The puppy Katie tried to protect," Mrs. Carrington said. "The one I saw Carson, your coachman, kick. I thought he'd certainly kill him if he could. And I think he would unquestionably have done so if Jimmy, the Grenville groom, hadn't agreed to let the puppy stay in his room in the loft."

Mr. Lacey got up. "Katie, would you please take me down to the cellar where you have the groom and the dog?"

Katie's mind was blank as she took Mr. Lacey down the stairs first to the kitchen floor and then to the cellar underneath. She was somehow past feeling frightened. It was only as she was turning the corner of the stairs on the last flight down that she realized that not only Mr. Lacey, but Mrs. Carrington, Master Christopher, and his two sisters were also following her.

Jimmy, who'd been sitting on the floor, jumped up when Mr. Lacey, followed immediately by Katie and Mrs. Carrington, reached the cellar. He stared at Mr. Lacey, who looked back. Finally Mr. Lacey said, "I've been told you're one of the Grenville grooms. Is that right?"

"Yes, sir."

"But they didn't take you to the country?"

"No, sir. They have grooms there and they want somebody here who can tend the horses when Mr. Grenville brings the coach or rides back in." He hesitated, then added, "I'm sorry about the barking. The dog got away from me for a moment. Don't be angry at Katie. If she's going to get in trouble, I'll leave."

Jimmy, Katie noticed, now had the cord around Paddy's neck to prevent the puppy from flinging himself at Katie.

Mr. Lacey looked at him. "What was his name?" he asked.

"Paddy, sir."

"No Irish there," Mr. Lacey said drily.

Feeling movement behind in the small, close cellar, Katie turned. Mrs. Alberts had joined them.

The cook raised her voice. "I've told Katie that she has no right at all to take our food out to this mongrel, but she takes it anyway. And I can assure you, sir, that if I'd had any idea she'd brought a strange black man and a dog into the house — "

"I'm delighted she did, Mrs. Alberts. Do you know what they're doing to negroes in the city now?"

"Yes, but I'm sure there was something else Katie could have done — "

"Such as what?" Mr. Lacey said.

"It's the new Irish immigrants who are causing all this trouble."

"True. But they're not the only ones." He glanced up at his mother-in-law. "Don't you agree, Mamma?"

"Absolutely right."

"Well, really, sir — " Mrs. Alberts said.

He turned back to Jimmy. "Please, by all means, stay here until the soldiers have come into the city and restored order. I'm delighted that someone in my household has been of help."

"And Paddy?" Jimmy asked.

Mr. Lacey looked down at Paddy, who, now free, was flinging himself at Katie.

"And Paddy — at least for the time being."

The rioting continued one more day.

Jimmy and Paddy, who was now free, more or less, to bark, remained for protection in the cellar, and Katie was able — under the glare of Mrs. Alberts's obvious but silent disapproval — to take food down.

Then, late on the fourth night and early the next morning, weary soldiers, who had marched without rest from Gettysburg in Pennsylvania, arrived and put down the riots. After four days of looting, burning, killing and hanging, the bloodied city was finally restored to some degree of peace.

Later that day, Mrs. Carrington summoned Katie. When she entered the back parlor where Mrs. Carrington was sitting, Katie was astonished to find Paddy sound asleep on the rug.

"Paddy!" she said.

The dog awoke, jumped up and, as always, flung himself at Katie.

"I don't know what to do about him, ma'am," Katie said. "I know you — you and Mr. and Mrs. Lacey were very kind. But I don't know what would happen to him if he goes back to the mews where Carson and the others can get at him if Jimmy isn't there."

"I thought after all I might adopt him," Mrs. Carrington said. "I'll talk to Mrs. Alberts."

Katie flushed. "That'd be very kind of you, ma'am."

"And I also thought I'd ask my daughter if she could spare you from the kitchen to become my personal maid. That way Mrs. Alberts could bring in her niece and the tensions there might be lightened. We could — well, we could go on with the lessons I was talking about." She glanced up at Katie. "It has to be your choice. But I think it would be a great shame to waste anyone with your spirit and intelligence on washing dishes. If you . . . if you were educated, you could be a teacher — or who knows? Anything else within reason you wanted. What do you think?"

It was almost too much to take in. Despite herself, Katie's eyes filled up. She looked at Mrs. Carrington and was suddenly overwhelmed by the distance between them. She swallowed and said, "I'm very grateful to you, ma'am."

It was true. And of course she wanted to accept. Learning to read? Not having to be a scullion all her life?

Mrs. Carrington was watching her. "Even though you don't like being the object of someone's help, isn't that right?"

For a moment Katie wondered what it would be like to talk to this lady as an equal. "Yes," she said finally, and added, "ma'am."

Mrs. Carrington got up. "Well, you can refuse. It's your choice, Katie." She went to the door and turned, smiling a little. "Let me know what you decide."

Katie knew before Mrs. Carrington left the room what she wanted to do, and went after her. "Mrs. Carrington, ma'am," she said.

Mrs. Carrington turned and smiled. "Yes, Katie?"

Katie took a breath. Her heart was pounding. "I do want to," she said.

When Jimmy left, he thanked everyone in the kitchen and said he'd like to thank Mr. Lacey in person.

James grumbled, but decided that after all the fuss about Jimmy, he'd better take him upstairs to where the master was reading in the back parlor.

"I came to thank you," Jimmy said. "You saved my life."

Mr. Lacey got up. "Katie did that, Jimmy. But I'm glad she did and I'm glad you're safe."

When Jimmy returned to the kitchen, Katie didn't

seem to be anywhere. He loitered a moment, then said, "Where's Katie?"

"Out back, taking the rubbish," Mrs. Alberts said. Like James, she felt she had to be civil.

Jimmy left by the kitchen door and met Katie returning to the house.

"There's no way I can thank you enough, Katie," he said.

Katie felt suddenly embarrassed, almost tearful. "Ach well, Jimmy, you saved Paddy." She paused, then burst out with something that had been on her mind. "It's a terrible thing that's happened . . . and it's worse, because it's the Irish. But not all the Irish, Jimmy. Brian, me brother, would have nothing to do with it. He says it's one of the reasons he wants to go West."

He said steadily. "That's all right, Katie, I know it's not all the Irish."

She glanced at him. "And what are you going to do now?"

Jimmy shrugged. "I guess go on being a groom. But, sometimes . . . sometimes I think it'd be nice to write a book like — Frederick Douglass did. Mr. Lowell told me he'd like me to do that, telling what my mother said about life as a slave."

"Mrs. Carrington said she was going to teach me to read. Maybe one day, if you do write a book, I can read it."

He grinned. "That'd be nice. Something to push

me on." They looked at each other for a moment, and he held out his hand.

Feeling awkward, she took it.

"Anyway, Katie," he said, "with any luck, we'll both be free."

About the Author

Isabelle Holland is the author of fifty books for children and adults, including *The Journey Home*, which *Booklist* described as full of "wonderful, complex and distinct characters. . . ." The daughter of a foreign service officer, Ms. Holland was born in Basel, Switzerland, and grew up around the world, spending many years in Guatemala and England.

When asked if something in her own family background prompted her interest in the New York City draft riots, Ms. Holland said not to her knowledge: Her Tennessee forebears came from England, Scotland and Wales — not Ireland, and those who fought in the Civil War were Confederates.

But having lived in New York City for many years, she has become fascinated with its history. She shares her home there with four engaging cats.

point®

Other books you will enjoy, about real kids like you!